Unpack this satchel of stories and you will find . . . an uproarious class trip to the Safari Park, some very unusual sum cards for a Maths lesson, a 'horrible' alphabet, a dog who becomes a teacher, a new boy with an uncanny gift, a charming country school from a long time ago, and a host of other fascinating and exciting characters. You won't want to stop reading until you get right to the bottom of the satchel!

No story has been put in the satchel without very careful inspection by children's book specialist Pat Thomson. All the stories are tried and tested favourites, and all by top children's authors – Joan Aiken, Anne Fine, Robin Klein, Dick King-Smith, Jan Mark and many others.

PAT THOMSON is a well-known author and anthologist. Additionally, she works as a lecturer and librarian in a teacher training college – work which involves a constant search for short stories which have both quality and child-appeal. She is also an Honorary Vice-President of the Federation of Children's Book Groups. She is married with two grown-up children and lives in Northamptonshire.

Also available by Pat Thomson,
and published by Corgi Books:

A POCKETFUL OF STORIES FOR
FIVE YEAR OLDS

A BUCKETFUL OF STORIES FOR
SIX YEAR OLDS

A BASKET OF STORIES FOR
SEVEN YEAR OLDS

A SACKFUL OF STORIES FOR
EIGHT YEAR OLDS

A CHEST OF STORIES FOR
NINE YEAR OLDS

A STOCKING FULL OF CHRISTMAS
STORIES

A SATCHEL

of School Stories

COLLECTED BY PAT THOMSON

Illustrated by Doffy Weir

CORGI BOOKS

A SATCHEL OF SCHOOL STORIES
A CORGI BOOK 0 552 52738 6

First published in Great Britain by Doubleday,
a division of Transworld Publishers Ltd

PRINTING HISTORY
Doubleday edition published 1992
Corgi edition published 1993
Corgi edition reprinted 1993, 1994

Corgi Books are published by Transworld Publishers Ltd,
61–63 Uxbridge Road, Ealing, London W5 5SA,
in Australia by Transworld Publishers (Australia) Pty Ltd,
15–25 Helles Avenue, Moorebank, NSW 2170,
and in New Zealand by Transworld Publishers (NZ) Ltd,
3 William Pickering Drive, Albany, Auckland.

Printed and bound in Great Britain by
Cox & Wyman Ltd., Reading, Berks.

Acknowledgements

The editor and publisher are grateful for permission to include the following material in this anthology:

Joan Aiken, 'Broomsticks and Sardines' from *A Small Pinch of Weather* (Jonathan Cape Ltd). Reprinted by permission of A M Heath & Co Ltd.

Richmal Crompton, 'William and the School Report' from *William's Happy Days*, copyright 1930 Richard C Ashbee. Reprinted by permission of Pan Macmillan Children's Books.

Anne Fine, 'Fabric Crafts' first published in *The Trick of the Tale* edited by Julia Eccleshare (Puffin Books), © Anne Fine 1990. Reprinted by permission of Murray Pollinger Literary Agent.

Iris Grender, 'The Really Small Girl in our Class' from *Did I Ever Tell You About My Birthday Party?* (Hutchinson Junior Books), © Iris Grender 1983. Reprinted by permission of Random Century Group Ltd.

Margaret Joy, 'Class Trip' from *You're In the Juniors Now*, text © Margaret Joy, 1988. Reprinted by permission of Faber & Faber Ltd.

Gene Kemp, Chapter 10 from *The Well*, retitled as 'Sixty Years Ago' for this publication, © Gene Kemp 1984. Reprinted by permission of Faber & Faber Ltd.

Dick King-Smith, 'Just a Guess' reprinted from *The Methuen Book of Strange Tales*, © Dick King-Smith 1980. Reprinted by permission of A P Watt Ltd.

Robin Klein, 'Hey, Danny!' from *Ratbags and Rascals*, text © Robin Klein 1984. Reprinted by permission of the publisher, Jacaranda Wiley Ltd.

Sheila Lavelle, 'Show and Scream' from *The Fiend Next Door*, published by Hamish Hamilton Children's Books, 1982, © Sheila Lavelle, 1982. Reprinted by permission of the publisher.

Jan Mark, 'The One That Got Away', © Jan Mark 1986, first published in *Story Chest: 100 Bedtime Stories* (Viking Kestrel, 1986). Reprinted by permission of Murray Pollinger Literary Agent.

Christine Nostlinger, 'The Dog Goes to School' from *A Dog's Life*. Originally published in German in 1987 as *Der Hund kommt!* by Beltz Verlag, © 1987 Beltz Verlag, Weinheim and Basel. This translation © 1990 by Andersen Press Limited. Published by kind permission of Andersen Press Ltd.

Frank Rodgers, from *A is For Aaargh!* (Viking Kestrel, 1989), © Frank Rodgers 1989. Reprinted by permission of Penguin Books Ltd.

Laura Ingalls Wilder, Chapters 20 and 21 from *On the Banks of Plum Creek* retitled 'Prairie School' for this anthology only. Reprinted by permission of Methuen Children's Books.

CONTENTS

Show and Scream

Angela isn't always horrible to me, though. Sometimes she's very kind and generous. She lets me ride her lovely new yellow bike whenever I want to, and I can read her comics every Saturday after she's read them first. I'm not allowed to buy comics because my mum doesn't approve of them and I don't think it's a bit fair. They're no worse than some of the soppy magazines she reads with all that awful love stuff and Mary Moan's Problem Page. My dad tells her it wouldn't do her any harm to read a good book for a change, but my mum says what about him and his football paper and that shuts him up.

Every morning in term-time Angela calls for me and we walk to school together, even though we're not allowed to sit together in class.

Miss Bennett always used to say we brought out the worst in each other. And even in Miss Bridge's class we've been put at opposite sides of the room. I have to sit next to that awful spiteful cat Delilah Jones, and Angela doesn't seem to mind a bit. She sits next to David Watkins, and he's the nicest boy in the class. I wouldn't even mind marrying David Watkins when I grow up.

I shouldn't have told Angela that, though. She went and spread it round the whole school. She even chalked it on the wall of the boys' loos, 'Charlie Ellis loves David Watkins'. And now he goes as red as a pillar box whenever I speak to him.

Angela is going to marry Prince Edward when she grows up because she wants to be a princess. She used to like Prince Andrew, but he went and married Fergie. I was glad when that happened, because Angela gave me all her scrapbooks with his photos in. My dad told her she was fickle, but she only laughed.

Anyway, we hadn't been in our new class five minutes before Angela started getting me into trouble. And it was a bright idea of Miss Bridge's that caused the whole thing. She's one of those keen and with-it teachers straight out of

college and crazy about Projects and Activities
and Learning by Experience and stuff like that.
She doesn't just write things on the blackboard
and make you copy them while she dozes at her
desk like all the other teachers do. It makes you
wonder what some of them get paid for sometimes.

The lesson was Nature Study, and we were
all a bit bored and sleepy because it was Friday and a warm September afternoon. I was
wishing the lesson was over so Angela and I
could go blackberry picking on the common.
I'd promised my mum I'd try to get enough
to mix with some of our apples for a pie. She
makes lovely blackberry and apple pies, my
mum does, with the sort of pastry that melts
in your mouth and loads of thick cream. No
wonder my dad's getting so fat.

Miss Bridge was talking about pets, and she
was asking the children in the class about the
different sorts of animals they kept at home and
what they fed them on and that sort of thing.

'Please, Miss Bridge, we've got a dog called
Hector,' said that fat Laurence Parker, putting
up his hand. 'We used to have a goldfish as
well, but we had to get rid of it because of the
noise.'

We all stared at him and somebody started to snigger. Miss Bridge's eyebrows nearly disappeared into her fringe.

'The goldfish made too much noise?' she said. 'Surely not.'

'No, Miss,' said Laurence. 'The dog did. It kept on barking at the goldfish.'

We all giggled like anything and even Miss Bridge had to smile. Then when we'd calmed down a bit she turned to me.

'What about you, Charlie?' she said. 'Have you got a pet?' And of course I'd been dreading that question because my pet isn't anything to boast about, but it's the only kind my mum will let me have as she can't bear animals' hairs all over the place.

'Well . . . um . . . er . . . I've got a tortoise,' I said at last.

'How nice,' said Miss Bridge politely, in that special grown-up sort of voice that really means 'how boring'. 'Is it a girl or a boy?'

Well honestly, what a stupid question. How is anybody supposed to tell whether a tortoise is a boy or a girl? I certainly can't tell the difference, and my mum and dad can't tell the difference, and I bet you anything that Miss

Bridge couldn't tell the difference, either. Even the vet has trouble.

'We think it's a boy,' I said, hoping she'd leave it at that. But this wasn't my lucky day.

'And what is his name?' went on Miss Bridge relentlessly. The question I'd been dreading most of all.

There was a muffled splutter of laughter from somewhere behind me and I knew it was Angela because she's the only one who knows. Everybody was waiting and I went all pink and hung my head and shuffled my feet and said nothing.

'What's the matter, Charlie?' said Miss Bridge, getting a bit impatient. 'You haven't forgotten your own pet's name?'

I was just making up my mind to tell a fib and say Fred or George or something like that when there was the sound of a chair scraping on the floor and Angela stood up.

'Please, Miss Bridge,' she said, and she could hardly speak for giggling. 'I know what Charlie's tortoise is called. Charlie's tortoise is called ROVER!'

I could have killed her. Everybody hooted with laughter and in the end Miss Bridge had to bang on her desk lid with the blackboard ruler. And then I had to explain all about my mum not letting me have a dog because of hairs on the carpets, so a tortoise called Rover seemed the next best thing.

And to my surprise Miss Bridge was quite sympathetic.

'I quite understand, Charlie,' she said gently, even though her mouth was twitching and I could tell she was dying to laugh, too. 'Perhaps you'll be able to have a dog later on. When you are old enough to look after it yourself.'

'Yes, Miss Bridge,' I said. 'I hope so.' I sat down thankfully and did my best to ignore the rude faces that awful Delilah Jones was making at me.

'Well now,' said Miss Bridge, smiling round at the class. 'This little chat has given me a good idea. The next few Fridays can be Pet Afternoons. I'll choose one person each week to bring their pet to school. And they can prepare a little talk about it for the rest of the class.'

You should have heard the moans and groans, and one or two people called out that they had no pets at all. Miss Bridge held up her hand.

'The animal doesn't have to be your own,' she said. 'I won't mind if you borrow one from

6

a relative or a friend. Try to get hold of some interesting, unusual sort of pet. But of course you must be sensible. We don't want donkeys or Saint Bernard dogs in the classroom.'

'Oh, Miss,' said Laurence Parker, sounding all disappointed. 'Can't I bring my killer whale?' And this time even Miss Bridge joined in the laughter. Laurence Parker does say some funny things sometimes.

'I'd really rather you didn't, Laurence,' said Miss Bridge, when the noise died down. 'But you can be first with your pet next Friday. We shall all be looking forward to a nice, interesting talk.'

The bell went for the end of afternoon school and Miss Bridge dismissed us. We all went trooping out, and Angela and I collected our belongings from the cloakroom.

'I hope Miss Bridge doesn't pick me for one of her Pet Afternoons,' I said gloomily, as we set off towards the common. 'I'd die if I had to bring Rover to school. I'd feel a proper fool.' Angela pushed her arm through mine.

'Well, I hope she chooses me,' she said. 'I wouldn't mind a bit.'

I stared at her in surprise.

'Why not?' I said. 'All you've got is a

7

jamjar with a dead caterpillar in it. I don't call that very interesting or unusual.'

She let go of my arm and began to hopscotch along the pavement.

'You know my Uncle Quentin who went to Oxford to study zoology?' she said over her shoulder. 'Well, he's got a job now at the London Zoo. And they often lend animals for things like school projects. I bet he could get me a nice little baby monkey or something.'

'He couldn't,' I said. 'You're making it up. How could he bring it all the way from London Zoo?'

'I bet he could,' she said. 'He only lives at Barlow. He could call with it on his way home. I'm going to ask him, anyway. So there.' And she went skipping off, leaving me to trudge dolefully along behind.

The next Friday came round and Laurence Parker turned up with a box of silkworms. You might not think silkworms are all that exciting, but he made his talk so interesting that everybody got fascinated with the funny little creatures and we were having such a great time that the afternoon was over before we knew it.

After that we had terrapins, a baby rabbit,

a cageful of stick insects, a talking mynah bird that kept saying a rude word over and over again until Miss Bridge had to put a cloth over its cage, and somebody even brought a tame hedgehog that snored loudly in its box all through the lesson. It didn't look as though Miss Bridge was going to pick me, after all, and I started to look forward to Friday afternoons.

Then it was Angela's turn, and she went home for lunch that day so she could pick up the animal her Uncle Quentin had brought. She wouldn't tell anybody what it was, not even me, and when she turned up in the afternoon with a small brown basket I could tell by her face that it was something very special.

And it was. Angela opened the lid of the basket and lifted out a sleepy, furry bundle with a long, black and white striped tail and a little pointed face with big ears.

'It's a ring-tailed lemur,' she said, smugly. 'His name's Ringo.' And everybody fell in love with it at once.

You should have heard all the oohs and aahs. The lemur sat on Angela's shoulder while she gave her talk, and I think her Uncle Quentin must have given her some help with that as well because she could never have made it up

9

herself. It was all about marsupials and the rain forests of Madagascar and it was just as good as David Attenborough on the telly.

Miss Bridge was as pleased as anything and she let everybody stroke the lemur before it went back into its basket. It was the friendliest creature you ever saw, because it had once been somebody's pet before it went to live in the zoo, and I couldn't help wishing I could keep it for myself.

'Thank you, Angela,' said Miss Bridge, beaming all over her face. 'A charming animal, and a most interesting talk. I'm delighted that you all seem to be responding so well to this project. Now, we just have time for one more pet before we break up for half term.'

Her eyes swept around the class and my heart sank because I suddenly knew who she was going to choose.

'Charlie Ellis,' said Miss Bridge with a smile. 'We haven't had your little pet, have we?'

I did my best to argue myself out of it, but she wouldn't listen.

'Tortoises are extremely interesting creatures,' she said. 'And I know you can make

10

your talk well worth listening to. I don't want to hear any more excuses.'

And so that was that. I felt really fed up, I can tell you. Even though Angela let me carry the basket with the lemur in it on the way home.

'How can I possibly take Rover to school?' I said in despair. 'Can you imagine it? They'll all laugh their silly heads off. Especially that fat Laurence Parker and that spiteful Delilah Jones.'

Angela put her arm round my shoulders.

'Cheer up, Charlie,' she said. 'I could always get my Uncle Quentin to borrow something for you, too.'

I stopped dead in the middle of the pavement and stared at her. I could hardly believe my ears.

'Do you think he would?' I said breathlessly.

'I don't see why not,' she replied, pushing her hair back from her face. 'He's coming over tonight to collect Ringo. I'll ask him then if you like.'

Well, when Angela came round later that evening to tell me that the answer was yes, I was so pleased and excited and relieved and grateful that I could have hugged her.

'That's all right, Charlie,' she said carelessly.

'You know what they say about a friend in need. But you can do my maths homework for me in exchange, if you like.'

I told my dad about it when we were having supper that night, and my dad said I should watch it. Angela Mitchell could be up to something, we all know what she's like, he told me. But my mum said it was wrong of him always to think the worst of Angela, and maybe she really meant to be a good friend this time. That made my dad choke on his sausages and mash, and I had to bang him on the back for five whole minutes.

And of course I should have listened to him because he's usually right, especially about things like that, but I went blithely off to bed and dreamed about all the lovely things that Angela's Uncle Quentin might bring me from the zoo. It could be a bush-baby, I thought, or a nice little owl, or even a koala bear.

But the week went by and Thursday came and still I hadn't found out what sort of animal I was getting. Angela's uncle was away at a conference for a few days, she said, and wouldn't be back until Friday morning.

'He's bringing the animal to my house at

lunch-time,' she explained. 'I'll go home for lunch and pick it up for you.'

'That's no good,' I said crossly. 'How am I supposed to prepare a talk when I don't even know what it's about?'

'I'm sorry, Charlie,' she said, and she really sounded as if she meant it. 'It's the best I can do. Do you want to forget the whole thing and just bring Rover instead?'

I shook my head hurriedly.

'Not likely,' I said. 'Anything but that. I'll just have to manage somehow.'

And on Friday afternoon of course Angela was late for school. The bell had gone and we were all in our places and I was worried half out of my wits when she came rushing breathlessly in and pushed a smallish wooden box into my hands.

'What is it?' I hissed frantically, but the teacher was coming into the room so Angela had to slip away to her place and sit down.

'Good afternoon, everybody,' said Miss Bridge, and we all clattered to our feet.

'Good afternoon, Miss Bridge,' we chorused politely. Then we all sat down again and the lesson began.

13

I stared at the box on the desk in front of me. It was about the size of a shoe box and it had a sliding lid with air holes drilled through. I was relieved that it looked so small. At least Angela hadn't brought me a crocodile.

I inched back the lid just a fraction and tried to peer inside, but it was all dark in there and I couldn't make out a thing. Then Miss Bridge's voice made me jump.

'Charlie! You're keeping us all waiting,' she said. So I got up and carried the box to the front of the class.

Everybody went very quiet and gazed at me expectantly. I looked at Angela hoping she would give me some sort of a clue, but she kept her head down and I couldn't see her face. I cleared my throat nervously. The room was so silent you could have heard a feather fall.

'Er . . . um . . . well,' I stuttered. 'This animal is a . . . ' I slid open the lid of the box and the whole class craned forward to look.

I think it was one of the horriblest moments of my life. I went stiff and cold all over and the hairs on the back of my neck went prickly and I shuddered with fright as I stared down at the THING in the box.

It had an ugly black furry body and an

ugly black leathery face and great nasty black
wings with claws on the ends. It was the ugliest
creature I had ever seen.

'Ugh! It's a BAT!' I said, and my voice
came out all croaky.

Angela knows there are two things I can't
stand at any price. One of them is spiders, and
the other is bats. They make me go all funny
just to look at them, and it's no good anybody

telling me that they're perfectly harmless little creatures. I can't help it if they make me think of graveyards and vampires and Dracula and blood and witches and dark cobwebby towers and creepy things like that. I imagine their claws tangled in my hair and their sharp little teeth biting my neck and I go goose-pimply all over and my dad says I read too many spooky books.

Anyway, this bat must have been disturbed by the light because it suddenly stretched out its great black wings and hopped out of the box on to my wrist. I felt its cold claws gripping my skin and that was the last straw. I dropped the box with a clatter and started to scream my head off.

'Blimey! It's a bloomin' vampire!' shouted that fat fool Laurence Parker, and that started everybody else off screaming, too. And it was sheer bedlam in the classroom with everybody leaping out of their desks and charging about bumping into one another and fighting to get to the door and diving under tables and things. And the bat made things ten times worse by swooping about and banging itself into the walls and windows and Miss Bridge didn't help much by yelling and thumping on her desk but there was so much noise that nobody took any notice of her anyway.

And of course in the end it was Angela who did the sensible thing. She climbed up on to the window-ledge with the box in her hands and sort of scooped the bat into it from the corner of the glass. Then she shut the lid and put it safely back on the teacher's desk.

Miss Bridge was standing there with her arms folded grimly and her face all red and I could tell she was furious. Everybody started shuffling back to their places with sheepish little grins and of course most of them hadn't been frightened at all but just thought it was a good excuse for a bit of a riot.

We all had to stay silent for the rest of the lesson and Miss Bridges made us write a composition about Self Control. I was more relieved than sorry because I couldn't have given a talk on bats to save my life. But of course I got kept in after school and given a good telling-off about silly behaviour and causing a disturbance and stuff like that.

'It would have been better to have brought your tortoise,' said Miss Bridge crossly, 'than to risk that sort of panic in the classroom. Do try to think more sensibly in future, Charlie.'

Angela was waiting for me when I came out of the gate but I refused to speak to her. Even when she tried to explain that the bat was a harmless fruit-bat from South America and was as tame as a kitten. I shoved the box into her hands and said I never wanted to see it, or her, ever again. And this time I managed to keep my word for a whole weekend.

This story is by Sheila Lavelle.

Class Trip

'Are we going on a trip this term, Mr Tucker?' asked Kevin Wilson.

'We usually do in summer, don't we, Sir?'

Mr Tucker stroked his beard and looked at his class.

'Any suggestions, then?'

'Go down a coalmine, Sir.'

'Go to the theatre.'

'A trip in Concorde.'

'Climb Snowdon.'

'Go round a chocolate factory.'

'Watch the England footy squad training . . . '

Everyone had an idea. Mr Tucker nodded at them all, then said calmly, 'Our coach is already booked for next Friday. You'll be getting letters to take home about it tonight. We're going to the Simbwana Safari Park.'

The following Friday, everyone was in school. It was the first full attendance for weeks. Mr Farmer, the caretaker, leant on his broom handle and watched them pushing and shoving to get into the coach.

'Don't know why you're paying good money to go to a Safari Park,' he growled to Mr Tucker. 'You can see enough little beasts round here any day.'

'Well, yes, Mr Farmer,' said Mr Tucker. 'But the ones we're going to see are quite wild.'

'That's what I meant,' muttered Mr Farmer.

By now everyone was in the coach. Mr Tucker stood at the front to count heads. 'Twenty-eight, twenty-nine, thirty . . . there should be thirty-one – who's missing?'

He opened the register and called all the names. They were all answered. Then he counted heads again – only thirty.

'This is ridiculous; who's missing?' he demanded.

'Perhaps it's me, Sir,' came a faint voice from near the back.

'It's Benjy, Sir,' said a couple of people

nearby. 'You didn't see his head, because he's bending down behind the seat.'

'Sit up, Benjy, for heaven's sake,' exclaimed Mr Tucker. 'What on earth are you doing behind there?'

'Having a nose-bleed, Sir,' came the faint voice again.

Mr Tucker raised his eyes to heaven.

'Keep your head back and your nose up,' he ordered.

He passed a wad of paper tissues back to Benjy, and nodded at the driver to get going. The coach soon left town and headed out through green countryside. It was already quite warm. After a while, the driver pulled into a lay-by to open the roof. He rolled up his sleeves and put on dark glasses before starting up again.

'It's going to be a scorcher,' he said.

'I hope it doesn't get too hot,' remarked Lucy, 'or the animals will lie under the trees to keep cool and we'll hardly see them.'

'There was an ace film on telly last night,' said Toothy Beddoes. 'About a place in Africa, where lions and things live – did you see it? There were these lions out hunting, see, and they closed in on a whole load of zebra, and they cut in and separated the straggler that couldn't keep up – a bit like One Man and His Dog, you know: when the sheepdogs get one on its own, then they run after it until it's tired out, and then they pounce on it and eat it.'

'I didn't know sheepdogs ate sheep,' said Lucy.

'No, dum-dum – the lions eat the zebra.'

'Do you think we might see them doing that today?'

'Eugh, no,' squeaked Belinda. 'We've had enough already today, with Benjy and his bleeding nose.'

'What's the matter with my bleeding nose?' demanded Benjy.

'Nothing, nothing at all – just keep your head back and your nose up in the air,' said Lucy hastily.

'But I'm fed up with looking at the ceiling like this,' protested Benjy.

'We'll tell you when there's something good to see outside,' said Shamila.

Conversation died down to a low murmur, interrupted only by a steady rustle of paper bags and chocolate wrappers.

'Can we start our lunch, Sir?' asked Shamila.

'Sounds as though most of you are well

stuck in already,' commented Mr Tucker. 'Don't forget, that's got to last you until we get home.'

'Don't worry, we've got plenty, Sir.'

'Yes, my mum used a whole loaf on my sarnies.'

'And my dad gave me a pound to buy crisps and chocolate to bring.'

'Ooh, 'tisn't half hot – wish we had some ice-cubes . . . '

This made everyone feel even hotter and stickier. But now the coach was approaching high wire gates over which hung a notice in enormous letters: Simbwana Safari Park. The children cheered. The coach stopped. Mr Tucker paid the entrance money, and the driver was given instructions at the cash desk. He stood up and shut the roof. Then he put the engine into a low gear and drove in through the gates. Slowly the coach rolled along an unfenced road into open country. A few clumps of trees were dotted here and there on both sides.

'It's just grass and bushes,' said Foxy.

They looked from side to side in disappointment; then Mary-Ann, who was sitting near the front, gave a piercing squeal.

'Look, look – elephants!'

They all shot round in their seats. From behind a distant clump of trees came a group of five elephants. Their ears waved to and fro as they ambled steadily towards the road.

'They're going to come right near us,' squeaked Mary-Ann.

Children at the back stood up and craned forward to see. Several people began to take pictures. The coach crawled forward and the elephants came on steadily.

'We'll run them over,' breathed Sylvia.

'No-one can run over elephants,' said Foxy.

The huge creatures stopped in the middle of the road only a few metres ahead and looked at the coach curiously, their trunks swaying as though in greeting. The children held their breath. Then the elephants turned their backs and plodded forward again.

'Ahh,' said everyone. 'That was brill – aren't they ace!'

'I'b habig anudder dose bleed, Sir,' called Benjy.

Mr Tucker passed back a second wad of paper hankies.

'It's the excitement,' he said. 'Just keep your head back, Benjy.'

Benjy obediently leant his head back and kept the wodge of tissues over his nose. He fixed his eyes on the roof of the bus. Suddenly his eyes widened and he called urgently:

'Bister Tucker, Sir, there's bunkeys od the roof!'

'Can't hear what you're saying, Benjy,' called back Mr Tucker; but by then everyone else was gazing up at the window in the roof, where two furry crouching figures could be seen. Two pairs of bright eyes stared down in amazement at the creatures in the coach below. They obviously thought the sight was

25

a funny one, for they turned and looked at one another as though in disbelief, then stared down again, flattening their noses on the glass. The excitement was too much for one of them, for a thin trickle of water began to drip down the outside of one of the windows.

'They're weeing on the roof!' shrieked everyone.

'Hey, you young monkeys,' shouted the driver, who had seen this in his mirror. 'I took this through the wash this morning – get off my coach!'

He pressed the windscreen spray button and started the windscreen wipers at their quickest speed. Some of the spray shot back over the roof of the coach and splashed on to the monkeys. They leapt back in surprise. Then, deciding that they'd seen enough, they swung down and lolloped away sideways over the grass, jabbering at one another and looking as though they were rocking with laughter.

The driver drove on, muttering to himself about his nice clean coach. From the back seats came a sudden click, then – ppsssshshshshshs . . .

'What was that?' asked Mr Tucker, not daring to look round.

'Oh, Sir . . . my drink
was a bit too fizzy, I
think it must have got
shaken up . . . could you
let me have some tissues to
wipe the roof, Sir . . . ?'

Mr Tucker handed back
another wad of paper hankies.
Then he lay back in his seat and
closed his eyes. The driver
drove on, scowling fiercely.
They came to some more high
gates and entered another
compound. Here the trunks of
the sparse trees were bare all
the way up, except for a
crowning topknot of foliage.
They soon realized why.

'Look – giraffes, over there!'

Once again they took
photographs and craned
their necks to see. There
were several giraffes,
a herd of zebra and
some deer.

'What's worse
than a giraffe with

a sore throat?' asked Tommy Pugh.

'Oh, a centipede with corns – that's an old one.'

In the next compound two Park Rangers drove past them in a Land Rover; they had rifles with them.

'What are they for?' asked Lucy nervously.

'Just for emergencies,' said the driver. 'You'd be surprised at the silly things people do. There was a chap here the other day, got a puncture – and got out to change the wheel, here in the lion compound! There'd have been a heck of a fuss if he'd been mauled . . . '

'What happens if *we* break down, then?' asked Toby.

'We just stay where we are and the Park Ranger patrols will soon spot us and get us towed to a safe place.'

'I'm roasting,' complained Mary-Ann. 'Why can't we open the window?'

'You saw those monkeys,' said the driver. 'They're quite likely to shove an arm through an open window and get you by the hair, or grab the ignition keys and run off with them – no thank *you*!'

The coach rumbled slowly along the dusty road, which was quivering in the heat. Under distant trees groups of lions lay unmoving in the shade.

'Look at that one yawning,' said Imran. 'I bet he's really bored.'

'Why did the Safari Park send for the Telecom man?' asked Tommy Pugh.

'Go on, I'll buy it,' said Mr Tucker with his eyes still closed, 'Why did the Safari Park send for the Telecom man?'

'Because they had a cross lion,' said Tommy.

'I think I'm going to be sick,' wailed Patsy.

'I told you not to bring six strawberry yoghurts,' said Lucy.

'We're nearly back at the main gate,' said Mr Tucker. 'Hang on, Patsy – we'll be getting out in a few minutes at the shopping area.'

Patsy managed to contain herself and the strawberry yoghurts, and soon the coach was turning into a huge car park.

'Be back in one hour prompt,' said Mr Tucker.

The class suddenly found new energy and clattered down the steps in search of postcards, souvenirs and more refreshment. An hour later they wearily hauled themselves back into the coach. Mr Tucker stood up to count heads before the journey home.

'Twenty-nine, thirty . . . that's funny, there should be thirty-one . . . oh no, where's Benjy?'

'Here, Sir,' came a faint voice from behind a seat.

Mr Tucker heaved an exasperated sigh.

'I suppose it's your bleeding nose again, Benjy?'

'No, Sir,' said Benjy. 'It's my bleeding knee. It's dripping on to my trainers. I was running to get in the ice-cream queue and I fell over.'

Without a word, Mr Tucker passed back a wad of tissues. He looked flushed and hot; his sleeves were rolled up and his shirt was open at the neck. He was fanning himself with the class register. He wearily nodded at the driver to start up. Some of the children hung over the back of his seat to show him what they had bought.

'Do you like my animal postcards, Sir? They're for my safari diary.'

'And I got a lion pencil sharpener – you stick the pencil in its mouth, see?'

'Look at my stick of rock: it says Simbwana all the way through – would you like a bite, Sir?'

'No thanks, Tommy,' said Mr Tucker. 'I don't really feel very hungry.'

'Look here – see what I got: it's a car sticker with lots of animals on,' said Foxy. 'We thought we could put it on the classroom window.'

'Oh yes?' said Mr Tucker.

'And look here,' said Imran. 'Under the picture it says, "We've been for a great day out at the Simbwana Safari Park."'

'Yes,' said Foxy. 'Well, we have, haven't we, Sir?'

Mr Tucker smiled.

'I'm glad you think so, Foxy,' he said. 'Really glad.'

This story is by Margaret Joy.

The Really Small Girl in Our Class

Although I was always small for my age, I wasn't the smallest in the class. There was a really small girl in our class and the first time I saw her I thought she must be much younger than the rest of us. I soon knew she wasn't.

We had an imitation birthday cake made of plaster of Paris.

Whenever someone had a birthday the right number of candles were put on to the cake and lit. Then the birthday boy or girl would stand on a chair holding the cake and looking a whole year older. The class would sing 'Happy Birthday to You'. It was a favourite song of ours so we always sang it very loudly.

One day it was Lucy's birthday. So our teacher put six candles on the cake and we all sang. Lucy was very small for six and it was hard to believe that she was having her sixth birthday before some of us who were much bigger than she was.

As well as being very small, Lucy was very quiet. She never chatted but just got on very quietly with her work. She didn't smile much either and seemed to like to play alone, so that was what we let her do.

Lucy was very very good at work. She read all the hard books and had to go to the head-mistress for some harder books. She always had lots of ticks in her sum book and stars in her writing book.

Lucy did everything with us but somehow she was always alone. Some children are like that. Perhaps it's because they don't want to chatter.

One day a strange thing happened to Lucy and it was because she was so small. A lady came into the classroom holding Lucy by the hand. Lucy looked cross.

The lady said, 'Look, I found this toddler in the playground – I think one of the mothers must have lost her. She's too small to be at school.'

Miss Clark our teacher explained that Lucy was just a bit small for her age and the lady went away. It was horrible for Lucy being mistaken for a toddler.

One day Lucy did something secret and funny and we all knew about it. It was really quite clever.

We had sausagemeat for school dinner. Instead of eating it, because it tasted simply awful, Lucy put hers into her pocket. That afternoon we did some clay modelling. Lucy did some clay modelling and when she had finished she took out the sausagemeat and modelled that into a teddy bear. Everyone left their model on the window-sill to dry. We all knew that we could paint our models as soon as they were dry. Lucy kept her teddy bear model in her pocket.

A week later all the models were dry so we mixed the paints. Then we painted our models. Lucy painted both her models. We all nudged each other as Lucy painted the sausagemeat teddy bear. Miss Clark our teacher didn't notice. All the models were put to dry again on the window-sill. This time the sausagemeat teddy bear was sitting there to dry as well.

Every day we all looked at the drying teddy bear. He looked fine for a long time. But then

he went mouldy. Fine green hairy mould began to grow all over him. A boy called Michael showed it to Miss Clark.

Miss Clark looked surprised. 'I didn't know that clay could go mouldy,' she said. 'Paint it again, Lucy, because we want to put it on display for Open Day.'

So Lucy painted the teddy again even though she knew the green mould wouldn't go away.

On Open Day all the parents saw the models, the paintings and all the work in our classroom.

I heard Lucy showing her sausagemeat teddy bear to her mother.

'Look,' she said, 'I made it from sausagemeat – it's gone mouldy.'

'Stop making up silly stories,' her mother answered. 'It's made from clay, everyone knows that.'

We all knew it was secretly made from sausagemeat and we all felt quite proud of the teddy bear sitting on the window-sill. It was quite green and very hairy. When we put our noses near, the smell was terrible. It was strange. All the children knew the teddy bear was made of sausagemeat but none of the grown-ups believed it.

We all thought Lucy should have had a prize for the green hairy teddy.

This story is by Iris Grender.

Charlie Plans a Maths Lesson

'I'm going to be a landlady,' said Mrs Robinson.

'What's a landlady?' asked Charlie, who was scraping up the last of his cornflakes.

'I know,' said Lucinda. 'You let rooms to people.'

'But we haven't any spare rooms,' said Charlie.

'There's Gran's room,' said his mother. 'I'm letting it for three weeks to a student teacher who is coming to your school for teaching practice. She was going to stay at the farm, but Mrs Ford is booked up with summer visitors, so I said we'd have her.'

'Is a student teacher someone who's learning to teach?' asked Lucinda.

'Yes,' said Mrs Robinson. 'Now, have you finished, you two? It's time to get the car out.'

As soon as they arrived at school, Lucinda ran off to tell her friends in the Top Juniors, where Sir taught, all about the student who was going to stay with them. Charlie joined the Lower Juniors, who were racketing about in the lobby, and swapped his Cadbury's Flake with Tim Crossman's Mars Bar before Miss Clarke called them into the classroom. She sat at her desk collecting dinner money, as she did every Monday morning. When she had taken Charlie's envelope, she told him to go and tidy the Nature Table.

'It's your turn today with Robert,' she reminded him.

Charlie and Robert were friends. They liked the same things and hated the same things. One of the things they hated was doing the Nature Table.

'Nature's silly,' said Robert.

'All flowers and growing beans and mustard and cress and all that muck,' said Charlie.

There were eight pots of very dead flowers, and the blotting paper had dried up round the runner beans. The bell for Assembly rang before they finished, so they left the flowers to droop still lower in their jars and filed out with the rest of the Lower Juniors into Sir's classroom.

As Charlie passed the piano, he managed to trip Lucinda, who was putting the hymn-book on its stand. She fell on to the keys and made a massive crash of discords that sounded like Stravinsky.

'Carefully, carefully,' said Sir, who hadn't seen exactly what happened. Lucinda glared at Charlie but he was looking the other way.

After prayers and a hymn, Sir told them about the student, and Charlie pricked up his ears.

' . . . She will be coming on Thursday to visit the school and get to know us. Then she will return to College, but later on she will be back for three weeks to do some teaching. I am sure you will do your best to make her welcome and that I can count on all of you not to let yourselves down by bad behaviour.' He paused to look hard at a few of the Lower Juniors, and Lucinda knew which ones he was looking at.

'Right,' he said. 'Lower Juniors, return to your class.'

Back in the Lower Juniors classroom the place buzzed with excitement, because Miss Clarke said that the student was going to teach them. There was more excitement when Charlie announced that the student would be staying in his house.

'Cor, I wouldn't like a teacher staying with me . . . oh sorry, Miss Clarke,' said Annie Thomas, who always put her foot in it. 'Why can't she go on living at the College?' she asked quickly.

'Because it's thirty miles away and too far for the coaches to get them all out to country schools like ours in time to be here at nine o'clock,' explained Miss Clarke.

Thursday came, and their student arrived in a minibus. Her name was Miss Thompson, and she and the Lower Juniors spent the morning getting to know each other. Annie Thomas thought she was 'ever so nice' and Carol Davies liked the way she did her hair. Charlie hated her. It was all because she asked to look at his English book. His English book was very private. He knew he couldn't spell and so did Miss Clarke, but he didn't see why he should let Miss Thompson into the secret.

'Where's your English book, Charlie?' she asked.

'Dunno,' said Charlie.

'Well, it can't be far, can it?' She began

poking around in Charlie's drawer.

Charlie stopped her. 'I'll look,' he said. He messed about in his drawer, turning books over and hoping she would go away. By mistake, the English book came up on top, and before he could send it to the bottom again, Miss Thompson pounced.

'Here it is,' she said and sat on his table turning the pages. At last she handed the book back. 'Thank you, Charlie,' she said. She opened her notebook and wrote a few things in it. All that Charlie could see was his name at the top of the page, then lots of writing he couldn't manage to read. She was probably writing about how dumb he was.

'What are your hobbies?' she asked after she had been writing for a bit.

'I dunno,' said Charlie.

If Miss Thompson had asked him what things he most liked doing, he would have known what she meant. He could have told her about fishing from the bridge with Robert and Tim, about collecting spiders and stones and shells and sticking pictures of his favourite pop stars in a scrapbook. But she didn't ask him that.

'Do you like reading?' she asked.

'No,' said Charlie.

'Do you like anything?' asked Miss Thompson.

'Spiders,' said Charlie, and he was going to tell her about his collection of super whoppers in the tool shed at the bottom of the garden when she turned away.

'She's daft,' said Robert, who had been listening in.

'I hate her,' said Charlie. 'I wish she wasn't coming to live with us.'

When Miss Thompson came to stay, later in the term, Mrs Robinson arranged for all the family to have a meal together in the evening. Charlie didn't say a word all through supper although his mother tried to include him in the conversation.

Miss Thompson had lots to say to his mother and father. She made them laugh when she told them funny things that happened at College, and she talked about the College tutors as well. These were the teachers whose job was to show the students how to teach. There was one she was really afraid of. Her name was Miss Follyfoot. If she thought her students weren't good enough, they had to leave College and find a different job.

On the way to school in the car next morning, Lucinda was very talkative. She described how the school was run by Mr McKay, 'Sir' to everyone except the teachers, and what the classes were like. The Top Juniors were the best, the Infants weren't bad for babies, and the Lower Juniors, in spite of having a good teacher, were the end, and she was sorry for Miss Thompson. Charlie glared, but said nothing.

Miss Thompson didn't take the whole class for lessons during the first week, only the top group, but she used to read a story to the class at the end of each day. She read about Robin Hood and sometimes let them act bits of it, and she chose Charlie to be Robin. Charlie grudgingly admitted to himself that she wasn't bad, and by the end of the week, he wished he was in the top group. They were doing all sorts of unusual things with her. They visited the church and went to the top of the tower with Mr Patterson the Vicar. Then they went round the graveyard to look at the tombstones, to find out which were the oldest. Twice they sat on the pavement outside the school and did traffic counts, and one afternoon Miss Thompson took them across to the village shop to buy flour, sugar, margarine, raisins and candied peel to make buns.

Charlie began to like Miss Thompson. She told him one day at breakfast that Miss Follyfoot had discovered some wrong spellings in her notebook.

'Can't you spell either?' asked Charlie.

Miss Thompson grinned. 'Not always,' she said.

Charlie could see that she was terrified of Miss Follyfoot, and each time her tutor came everything went wrong, even with Miss Clarke and all the top group willing it to go right.

It made Miss Thompson very miserable. 'She never comes to the good lessons,' she told Charlie's mother.

'You must stop being afraid of her,' said Mrs Robinson. 'Forget about her. Pretend she isn't there.'

'I can't,' said Miss Thompson. 'As soon as I see her I go all tight inside. I know everything will go wrong and it does.'

During her second week in school, Miss Thompson taught the whole class and they loved it. But they could be sure that if a science experiment failed to work or if paint water was spilt or an important book went missing, it would happen when Miss Follyfoot was there.

At the end of the week, Miss Follyfoot said she was coming in on the following Wednesday morning and she was bringing the Principal of the College with her.

'That must be because I'm so awful,' Miss Thompson told the Robinsons at tea-time. 'The Principal hardly ever goes out to see students unless there's something wrong with them.'

'What are you going to teach when they come?' asked Mrs Robinson.

'She says I've got to do a Maths lesson,' said Miss Thompson. 'I don't know what I shall do. Most of the class are doing individual work and need lots of help.'

'Do something they can all manage,' Charlie heard Miss Clarke say to Miss Thompson the next day. 'Like measuring. The top group understand about radius and diameters, so let them measure bicycle wheels on Wednesday and they can try to find out about circumferences. The middle group can have the big tape measures for doing perimeters and areas. Now the lower group are a bit of a problem . . .'

Then Miss Clarke noticed Charlie. 'You get on with your work card, Charlie,' she said. 'Miss Thompson will be with you in a moment.'

On Friday evening Miss Thompson began making a set of sum cards which the lower group could use the following Wednesday. Charlie watched her and thought they were very dull. Each card had two coloured lines of different lengths drawn on it. The lines were labelled A and B. Each card had a sentence which said: 'Measure line A and line B. Which line is longer and by how much?'

'Even the dumbies in the lower group will be bored out of their minds doing those,' said Charlie when he and Robert met in the Robinsons' tool shed later that evening.

'Well, we can't do anything about it. She'll have to fail, that's all,' said Robert.

'She can't fail. It wouldn't be fair,' said Charlie. 'She can teach all right when Miss Follyfoot isn't there.'

'Couldn't we capture her and tie her up and put her in the boiler house?' suggested Robert.

'Then she'd be sure to fail if she was tied up and couldn't teach,' objected Charlie.

48

'Idiot,' said Robert. 'I mean tie up Miss Follyfoot.'

'She's far too big,' said Charlie. 'Haven't you seen the size of her feet and those long dangling arms? She'd clobber us before we got the rope out and anyway she's bringing some Sir with her who runs the College.'

'All right,' said Robert. 'So what do we do?'

Charlie thought. 'Measuring wheels and the playground's all right. It's the sum cards which are going to fail her. We've got to do something about those sum cards.'

'What?' asked Robert.

'I dunno,' said Charlie, 'but they ought to be jazzed up a bit.'

The tool shed was gloomy and Charlie went outside. He leant against the side of the shed and put his hands in his pockets and scuffed the ground with one foot. Robert followed him out and they both crouched down to watch a couple of worms wriggling in the dust near Charlie's feet.

'Got it!' yelled Charlie, springing up and nearly trampling on the worms in his excitement.

'Got what?' asked Robert.

'The sum cards,' said Charlie. 'Instead of measuring lines they can measure worms.'

'It's much more difficult measuring worms,' said Robert. 'They don't keep still, especially if you try to line them up with a ruler.'

'That's all right,' said Charlie. 'Maths is supposed to be a difficult subject.'

'Where do we get the worms?' asked Robert.

'Dig,' said Charlie. 'There must be a million in this garden.'

'We'll need to keep them somewhere till Wednesday,' said Robert.

'In matchboxes,' said Charlie. 'I've got heaps upstairs.'

Robert started digging for worms while Charlie ran indoors for his matchboxes.

'I've got thirty-seven,' he announced, coming back with a bulging plastic bag. 'Let's get thirty-seven, all sizes.'

It took some time, but at last thirty-seven worms lay in thirty-seven matchboxes. Then it was bedtime, so they left the boxes in the shed under the work bench, hidden beneath plastic sacks.

On Saturday Charlie brought out his felt-tipped pens so that they could write numbers on the boxes. Later in the day they begged a couple of pieces of coloured card from Miss Thompson and took them to Charlie's bedroom, where they cut them into thirty-seven cards. It was hard work, and the writing took them all the rest of the day, with pauses for meals. Charlie looked through the cards when they had finished.

'They'll have to do,' he said.

'Your writing's all lopsided,' said Robert.

'Yours is like a spider's with a hang-over,' said Charlie. 'Let's have a look at the worms.'

The worm in the first box they opened looked dead even when Charlie poked it.

'What's wrong with it?' asked Robert.

They opened a few more boxes and all the worms in them looked as dead as the first.

'They were all right when we put them in,' said Charlie. 'I remember number twenty-eight especially. He was a fighter. Look at him now.' He flicked worm twenty-eight and it didn't trouble to squirm. It lay where his finger had put it.

'They'll be dead by Wednesday,' said Robert. 'Fancy making all those cards for nothing.'

'I know what's wrong,' said Charlie. 'They're drying up. Do you remember in the Infants? We put them in a wormery because Mrs Bray said that worms need to keep damp.'

'We can't wet the matchboxes, they'll rot,' said Robert.

'They'll have to go in my old aquarium,' said Charlie. 'With lots of damp earth. I'll get up early on Wednesday morning and put them back in their boxes. I always hear Miss Thompson's alarm.'

They found the aquarium and put the worms in it and, thanks to Miss Thompson's alarm, Charlie managed to get the worms re-boxed before breakfast on Wednesday. They had all survived after their spell in the wormery except number twenty-eight, which Charlie decided was clinically dead and threw out of the window.

In school, everyone could see that Miss Thompson was nervous. Miss Clarke reminded them that Miss Follyfoot was coming with another visitor from the College and asked them to be on their best behaviour. It was a very hot day, so the lower group took their tables and chairs to a shady part of the playground so that Miss Thompson could keep an eye on them while she was with the other two groups doing their practical work.

They had arranged themselves outside when a car drew up. Miss Follyfoot got out with a grey-haired, jolly-looking man and they went in together to see Sir. Miss Thompson gave out her sum cards to the lower group and explained what they had to do. She sent the middle group to start measuring the playground and then settled down with the top group, who were measuring bicycle wheels.

'Come on,' said Charlie.

He and Robert went over to the lower group, who were busily measuring lines A and B at their tables under the big chestnut tree. Out of the corner of his eye Charlie saw Miss Follyfoot and the Principal come to the school door. Robert was already collecting in Miss Thompson's cards and giving out the ones he and Charlie had made.

'You can work in two's if you like,' said Charlie as he handed round the matchboxes. 'And there are more cards and boxes,' he added, putting the spares on the ground beside Annie's table.

'Charlie and Robert, aren't you supposed to be measuring the door?' said Miss Thompson.

They hurried towards it and stepped politely aside as Miss Follyfoot came down the steps.

'It's all right,' she said. 'Go on with what you're doing. I've only come to watch. What are you . . ? ' She stopped because a scream from Annie Thomas came across the playground, followed by more screams from Carol Davies. There was sudden uproar from the whole lower group. Johnnie Norbut started to chase Susan Carter round the playground with two worms dangling from his fingers. Annie Thomas stood on her chair and Carol Davies demanded Miss Clarke at the top of her voice. A table was knocked over and Jenny Biggs was having hysterics, screaming that Christopher Dodds had dropped a worm down her dress.

Sir, Miss Clarke and Mrs Bray collided

in the doorway as they came to see what had happened.

'Hey!' yelled Charlie. 'Stop treading on those boxes. You'll kill the worms.' He ran over to where Johnnie Norbut was jumping up and down in front of Susan Carter, who was crouching behind the overturned desk screaming blue murder.

'Get your foot off those boxes,' shouted Charlie.

'You shut your mouth!' yelled Johnnie, giving Charlie a thump in the eye. Charlie landed a punch on Johnnie's nose and it began to bleed. Johnnie kicked Charlie and the two of them rolled over and over on the ground until they were lifted off each other by the Principal and Sir.

Charlie shook himself as well as he could while he was still being gripped in the Principal's firm hand. Then the school and the playground and the chestnut tree stopped whizzing round and everything came back into focus. Miss Thompson looked as if she was going to cry. Charlie didn't want to cry. He was mad. Mad with Johnnie Norbut for running about chasing people with worms instead of measuring them. Mad with the whole of the lower group for messing up the lesson and making Miss Thompson fail.

When order had been restored, it was Miss Follyfoot who asked Sir to let Charlie explain and the Principal seemed as interested as she was to hear his story. From the look in Sir's eye, Charlie knew that he wanted to slipper both him and Johnnie Norbut so hard that neither of them would be able to sit down comfortably for a week. But Sir had to be polite to visitors, so he sat and listened while Charlie told them how Miss Thompson had thought that Miss Follyfoot was going to fail her, and how he and Robert had worked so hard all weekend to make the lesson a success.

When he had finished, Sir punched his hands together. 'Well I'm da . . . er . . . well I'm blessed,' he said, and forgot all about slippering people.

The Principal was laughing and Miss Follyfoot had a grin on her face which made her look quite human. The Principal turned to Miss Thompson. 'If you can inspire such devotion in your pupils, you can't be that bad,' he said. 'Don't worry, no-one's going to fail you.'

Miss Follyfoot turned to Charlie and Robert. 'It was very kindly meant,' she said. 'But I think you had better let teachers plan their own lessons in future.' Her face changed. 'You weren't thinking of being teachers yourselves when you grow up?'

'No, Miss Follyfoot,' said Charlie and Robert in horror.

'Thank goodness for that,' said Miss Follyfoot.

This story is by Sylvia Woods.

Sixty Years Ago

I called for my friend Elsie from the post office and we got to school early and watched Gladys Clarke (the Head Girl) ringing the school bell in its little tower above the beams, ding, ding, dong, calling the children to school, until Mrs Packard strode in, filling the school with her big voice, her large round glasses and her big, tall self.

There were three teachers, Mrs Packard, the Headteacher, Miss Kitchen, the Junior teacher and Evie, the least teacher, in the Infants.

Elsie gave out Scripture books and I gave out the blue Ballard Arithmetic books, taking care to give ourselves clean ones with no scribble on them. Then we went out into the playground until Mrs Packard blew the whistle for us to come in. It was a square playground with lines and circles for drill marked on it and railings round the outside with chicken wire over them. We joined in the game of tag the Juniors were playing and ran up and down until Johnny Everton fell down, his feet caught up in the chicken wire, and lay there crying. We stood round and told him to get up, he wasn't hurting, and somebody started to laugh, and we all laughed for we thought Johnny was joking. Then Tom and Charlie Oxenbold came up and looked at Johnny, and Tom said, 'Fetch somebody quick instead of standing there laughing your heads off. Annie. Move.'

So I ran and fetched Evie, who came and picked Johnny up and carried him off.

And Charlie said, 'His arm's broken.'

And Tom said, 'I don't think much of you lot. Specially you, Annie.'

We had to line up and march into school and I felt like a worm, a nasty worm.

Gladys Clarke gave out the hymnbooks as we stood in the schoolroom, Juniors on one side and Seniors on the other, Mrs Packard, Miss Kitchen, two black stoves and a black-board in between. Evie was with the Infants, in their room, but with the door open. They sang, *There's a Home for Little Children*, said

Our Father, and then the door was closed and we had our hymn, though all I could think of was Johnny sitting in the stock room with a broken arm. Did broken arms ever get better or were they broken for ever? I wished I hadn't laughed.

Mrs Packard read a prayer and then we had to recite the Creed, *I Believe*, while she walked up and down, stopping suddenly and putting her ear to a mouth to see if that person was saying it properly, and if you didn't you had to stay in after school and say it to Mrs Packard *all on your own*. Then she went up to her high desk and seated herself. We waited.

'HARRY ROWLEY!' The name exploded in the room. 'Seven nines!'

An awful pause followed. Harry's mouth was moving but nothing was coming out of it, least of all the answer. But five people, including Tom, were all mouthing it at him.

'Sixty-three,' he gulped at last.

'Stanley Birch! How many pints in a gallon?'

'Eight,' whispered Stanley.

'Thomas Sutton! How many furlongs in a mile?'

I stood stiff as a poker, but eight he answered, just like that.

61

'Mary Cook. Spell psalm.'

'S–a–r–m, Mrs Packard.'

'Lizzie Bent?'

'S–a–l–m.'

'Annie Sutton. You spell it.'

What was happening? She never asked the Juniors. All the Seniors were looking at me across the space in the middle of the room. And Tom. I must get it right and then he'd forgive me for laughing when I shouldn't have.

'P–s–a–l–m,' I said. And Mrs Packard smiled which made me really scared.

'Some people know their spellings,' she said. 'Some Juniors if not Seniors.'

I smiled at Tom and he looked the other way. Lizzie Bent put her tongue out. As we went back to our seats Elsie said:

'You should've made out you didn't know. They won't 'arf be mad at you.'

It was a long morning. I was not HAPPY.

But worse was coming. The nurse came in with my glasses and fitted them on me, and showed me my face in a mirror. I looked awful. So did everybody else. They all had spots and cruckles on their faces which I'd never seen before.

No-one came near me at play-time. Not even Elsie. She'd got another friend.

'No wonder she's clever. Old Four Eyes, I mean. You have to be when you look as bad as that,' said Lizzie Bent.

Next day they had forgotten about me, for there was a new girl at school and she was pretty, with short, shiny hair, and a dress that had a low waist and press studs all down the back. It had a checked pattern and a short skirt and no-one had a dress like it. Her voice was different, too, clear and shiny, like her hair. Her dad was a doctor.

'I'll put her beside you, Annie, as you're at the same standard,' said Miss Kitchen, and when everyone crowded around her at play-time I was there and so couldn't be left out.

It was hot and we played skipping and she ran into the cloakroom with me to get a drink of water from the tap, and somebody tugged at her dress as she bent over the sink, and all the press studs popped undone, and I saw her back!

It was bare and brown, and knobbly down her spine. She wasn't wearing a liberty bodice.

She didn't have a liberty bodice. There were girls in the world who didn't wear liberty bodices.

'Come on, Annie,' she said. 'You can be my friend.'

'Even though I've got these glasses?' I asked.

'Oh, they don't matter. I've got to wear a brace on my teeth.'

'What's a brace?'

'For my teeth. To make them straight. You ought to have one too when you get older.'

'Oh. Tell me.'

'I'm not speaking to you, Annie Sutton,' Elsie called out.

I didn't bother to answer. I wanted to hear about straight teeth and how to get out of wearing a liberty bodice.

This story is by Gene Kemp.

The Dog Goes to School

The dog walked on for several days, keeping himself to himself. He might pass the time of day when he met someone, or exchange a few words with the landlord when he went into an inn, but that was all. After such a strenuous friendship as his friendship with the pig, a person needs peace and quiet. However, the dog was not bored, because he talked to himself so much. He used two voices, so that his conversations with himself wouldn't get monotonous. He asked himself questions in a deep, growly voice. And he answered them in a high, fluting voice. He looked at a great many things too. He liked looking at flowers, beetles and butterflies. He called it *taking photographs in his head*. In the evening, when he was in bed at an inn, he sorted out the photographs in his head. He had a whole album of them, filed away in proper order. Unfortunately, he didn't know the names of all the flowers, beetles and butterflies he saw. And he had no reference books to look them up in. So he gave all these things new names. He called one beetle Bold, and another beetle Mrs Miller. He called a flower Rudolph, and another flower Icing Sugar. He gave butterflies names like Dawn and Stripy Star. Best of all, however, the dog liked looking at stars. He filed them away in his head under names like Melancholy and Laughter, Black-and-Blue, Farewell, and *Au Revoir*.

One warm afternoon, the dog lay in a meadow for hours, taking photographs of feathery white cirrus clouds in his head. He didn't move until the sun had dipped below the horizon. He had been lying there so long that his back was stiff.

'Not lumbago, is it?' the dog asked himself anxiously.

'It could be,' he answered himself. 'Meadows always tend to be damp, and the damp doesn't do an old dog's back any good.'

'You think I ought to go and find a bed for the night pretty quick, then?' the dog asked himself.

68

'Quick as you can,' he replied. 'A stiff back needs a soft bed!' (Here the dog was wrong, because a stiff back needs a hard bed, but the dog didn't know much about medicine.)

So the dog set off in search of a bed for the night. All the rooms were taken in the first inn he came to. In the second inn he came to, the prices were too high for him. The third inn was closed for renovations. It was pitch dark by the time the dog got to the fourth inn. He heaved a sigh of relief when he saw a notice on the door saying *Rooms Available*. But just as he was about to open the door a fat man and a fat woman came out of it. The fat man was scratching his belly and the fat woman was scratching her bottom. 'Disgusting!' the fat woman told the dog. 'The health authorities ought to be notified,' the fat man told the dog. And then they told the dog that the rooms were full of bugs and fleas. They showed the dog bug and fleabites on their arms and legs.

The dog thanked them for the information and walked on. His back was getting stiffer and stiffer. He wound his woolly scarf round his waist, because wool is warm and warmth is good for a stiff back. The dog went on by the light of the moon until it was nearly midnight, and in spite of his woolly scarf his stiff back was bothering him more and more all the time. As well as that, he was exhausted. He decided that when he came to the next village he would ask for shelter for the night in the very first house he reached, whoever lived there.

It may not be the height of good manners, said the dog to himself, but if I don't get some sleep soon I shall drop in my tracks, and that won't do my back any good at all!

The first house in the next village happened to be the school. The dog walked around the school building shining his torch in through the windows. Two of them were classroom windows, there were lavatories behind another, and a desk and a chair behind a fourth. There didn't seem to be a school caretaker's flat with a school caretaker asleep in it anywhere. But there was a corridor window open at the back of the school.

If there isn't a soul in the building, said the dog to himself, climbing in through the open window, then I'm afraid I can't ask anyone's permission to sleep here.

The dog decided to sleep in the room with the desk, because it had a soft carpet on the floor. He made his bed under the desk, using the big green pouch as his pillow and covering himself up with his scarf and his coat.

Before he went to sleep, he thought: I'd better get well clear of here first thing in the morning, because you're not supposed to climb into strange buildings. The teacher might call the police and then I'd find myself in jail!

But it didn't turn out that way. First thing in the morning, the dog overslept. He didn't wake up until he heard a bell ringing very loud: the school bell going for the beginning of lessons. It took the dog a moment or so to recover from the fright the bell had given him, and then he peered cautiously out of his hidey-hole under the desk. He saw that the door of the room was open.

There were a lot of children surrounding a bear in the corridor outside. 'Please, Headmaster, is the new teacher coming this morning?' one of the children asked the bear.

'That's what they said,' said the bear. 'But it's already after nine, and teachers don't often turn up late on their first day at work, so something's probably gone wrong again!'

I'd better be off, thought the dog. I'll climb out of the window! And picking up his luggage

71

in his paws, he crawled out from under the desk.

His back was still very stiff. He intended to steal over to the window on the tips of his paws. In the usual way, the dog was very good at stealing silently around, but it's not an easy thing to do with a stiff back. The dog tottered, hitting the desk with his travelling bag and the chair with his case. There was a tremendous crash. The bear turned round, saw the dog and made straight towards him. 'Ah, there you are!' he said. 'Welcome to our school!'

He thinks I'm the new teacher, thought the dog. And as it is nicer to be mistaken for a teacher than a burglar, he didn't set the record straight.

'We're just a dwarf school here,' said the bear.

'Really?' said the dog. 'The children look the usual size to me.'

'Ha, ha! You're a real joker!' said the bear, slapping the dog on the shoulder. 'I like a teacher with a sense of humour. Your predecessor was a sourpuss. That's how come he ended up in hospital with gall trouble!'

'Poor fellow,' murmured the dog. He had no idea why the bear thought he was a joker.

'And which would you rather?' asked the bear.

'I don't mind,' murmured the dog, who had no idea what the bear meant by this either.

'Then I'll take the big ones and you take the little ones,' suggested the bear.

'All right,' murmured the dog, thinking: I suppose I shall find out what he's talking about in time.

'Old Sourpuss taught the bottom four classes,' explained the bear.

Now the dog knew what the bear meant by big ones and little ones. 'And how far had my distinguished predecessor proceeded with the syllabus?' asked the dog, very pleased with himself for bringing out such an educated sort of sentence.

The bear thought about it. 'Well,' he said, 'the first class was doing counting, the second class was learning its tables, the third class was learning multiplication and the fourth class had got to division. But the children will have forgotten all that by now. We've done nothing but sing songs since Old Sourpuss went sick. I can't teach eight classes at once!'

The bear led the dog to a classroom, where he saw twenty children sitting at their desks. The tiny ones were in the front row of desks, the slightly bigger ones in the second row, the

73

even bigger ones in the third row and the quite big ones in the fourth row.

'This is our temporary teacher,' the bear told the children. 'Mind you're nice to him!' And the bear waved to the children and left the classroom.

The dog stared at the children. The children stared at the dog.

The dog cleared his throat. 'Well, I'm the dog!' he said.

'I'm Ann,' said a little girl in the front row.

'Pleased to meet you.' The dog bowed to Ann.

'I'm Peter,' called a boy in the back row.

'Pleased to meet you.' The dog bowed again.

'No, he isn't Peter,' said the two girls in the third row. 'His name's Basil!'

'If he'd rather be called Peter, why not?' said the dog.

'Then I'd rather be called Carmen,' said Ann.

'OK, Carmen,' said the dog.

A boy in the second row of desks put his hand up.

'Yes?' asked the dog.

The boy stood up. 'If I pick a new name too, which name will be on my report, the old name or the new name?'

'I don't like reports,' said the dog.

'You mean we won't have reports any more?' asked the boy.

'Yes, I'm afraid you will,' said the dog. 'But your real teacher Old Sourpuss will be back by the end of term, and he'll write them.'

'Won't we have to learn anything with you, then?' asked the boy.

'People are always learning,' said the dog. 'There's no such thing as not learning. If you don't have to learn things with me, well, you'll realize later you learnt that there are some teachers you don't have to learn things from!'

The boy's jaw dropped in surprise. He stared at the dog, who did not like being stared at, so he said at once, not to the boy but to all the children, 'Suppose I tell you the things you could learn from me, and then you choose one of them?'

Now all the children's jaws dropped, and they all stared at the dog.

'Or would it be better if I learnt something from you?' asked the dog. He looked round the class, but no-one spoke up. 'Oh, all right,' sighed the dog. 'We'll just have to go on where Old Sourpuss left off!'

Of course the dog could count and multiply

and divide perfectly well. He even knew his tables up to thirty-seven times thirty-seven. The only trouble was that he didn't know how to teach children maths. And he hadn't the faintest idea how he was to explain several different things to several different children all at once. I must play for time, thought the dog, and he said, 'Get your maths exercise books out, please!' (This was what his own schoolteacher always used to say. There couldn't be much wrong with that, thought the dog.) But the children had not brought any exercise books to school. They had only brought their song-books, because they had done nothing but sing songs with the bear for the last few weeks.

It occurred to the dog that his youngest son used to like counting marbles. And it also occurred to the dog that cherries look much like marbles, and it happened to be cherry time.

'Is there a greengrocer's anywhere here?' asked the dog.

'At the far end of the village,' said Carmen Ann.

'Then we're going to visit it,' said the dog. He didn't ask the children if they wanted to first, because he thought: they only let their jaws drop and stare when you ask what they want to do!

The boy who was so interested in his report asked, 'What lesson is going to the greengrocer's?'

'Going there is traffic instruction, shopping is consumer education, and coming back is athletics, because we'll hop back on one leg!' said the dog.

The dog took the children through the village. He was unable to give them much traffic instruction, because there was no traffic about. Only a tractor coming towards them, driving bang in the middle of the road. So the dog told the children the tractor driver was an idiot. And he shouted to the tractor driver, 'Keep on the left, you fool!'

Before the dog took the children into the greengrocer's he went into the post office and had two pound coins changed into five-pence pieces.

'How many five pences have we got now?' he asked the children.

'Forty,' said a boy from the fourth class.

'And how many of you children are there?' the dog asked a girl in the first class.

77

'Don't know,' said the girl.

'Try counting,' said the dog.

The girl counted. She counted from one to twenty.

'And how many five-pence pieces will each of you get if there are forty of them and twenty of you?' asked the dog.

'Twice twenty is forty!' shouted a boy in the third class.

The dog nodded, and gave each child two five-pence pieces.

Then they went into the greengrocer's, where there were different varieties of cherries on sale: yellow, bright red and dark red cherries. The dog gave the children a lesson about cherries. Sweet cherries and cooking cherries, rotten cherries and worm-eaten cherries, chemically sprayed cherries and organically grown cherries.

The lady in the greengrocer's did not care for that. 'Are you saying I sell rotten cherries?'

she asked suspiciously. And when the dog told the children to taste the different varieties of cherries so that they could make up their minds which they liked, the lady got very cross. 'I can do without customers like you!' she shouted.

'My dear madam,' the dog told the lady, 'we're not customers, we're a school class having a lesson.'

'Having a lesson in my shop?' said the lady, astonished.

'Of course,' said the dog. 'Fruit and vegetables are part of everyday life. It's important for the children to learn about that.'

So the lady said no more. She meekly weighed out eight pence worth of cherries per child, took their five-pence pieces and gave them pennies back. She didn't even grumble when the dog told the children, 'Mind you count your change, because people think it's easy to cheat a child!'

Then the children and the dog hopped back to school, thirteen hops on the right leg and thirteen hops on the left leg in turn. As the sun was shining, the dog kept the children out in the playground and taught them how to spit cherry-stones.

Tarzan James from the fourth class won the long-distance cherry-stone-spitting. He spat a distance of twelve metres, seventeen centimetres, three millimetres. Unfortunately, all the cherries were finished now, and there wasn't a single one left for an arithmetic lesson.

Never mind, thought the dog, the children have counted money and children, divided five-pence pieces by children and multiplied children by five-pence pieces in the post office! They've checked change in the greengrocer's, noted cherry-stone-spitting distances down to the nearest millimetre and learnt a progression of thirteen hopping home. That's enough maths for one day! 'School's over for today,' the dog told the children.

The children went home, and the dog picked up the cherry-stones, which hurt his back rather, since it was still a bit stiff. But the dog knew children don't like tidying things up. And he knew children don't like people who make them tidy things up.

And somehow or other – he didn't know just why – he wanted the children to remember him kindly.

Then the dog left the school. He found a

pretty inn in the village square, hired a room and got into bed, for the sake of his back. He wanted it to be better by next morning, so that he could go on walking at a good brisk pace.

Next morning, the dog's back was quite all right again. And the dog was ravenously hungry. He went downstairs and ordered breakfast: eggs and bacon, cheese, coffee, toast and raspberry jam.

The dog ate his breakfast with relish, with the map spread out on the table in front of him.

He wondered which way to go.

He decided to go south, because there was a large lake marked on the map, only about a day's walk away. All kinds of things go on at lakesides, thought the dog. I could make myself useful there. I could be a tourist guide dog. Or a life-saving dog.

When the dog looked up from his map, he saw Carmen Ann from the front row of desks and Lolita Jane from the third row of desks standing in front of him.

'What on earth are you doing here?' asked the dog, in alarm.

'We're the landlord's daughters,' said Carmen Ann, and Lolita Jane said, 'We'll all have to start for school now; it's nearly nine!'

'You two run on ahead,' said the dog, blushing, because he was ashamed of his deception. But you couldn't see that, because his face had hair all over it.

'We can't be late for school until you get there yourself, anyway,' Carmen Ann pointed out.

'I'll catch up with you,' said the dog. 'I run faster!'

'Bet you can't,' said Lolita Jane. 'We're the fastest runners in the district. Nobody catches up with us!'

And the landlord called out, from the bar, 'That's right! I don't say you can't run fast, Mr Teacher, but my daughters will beat you and no mistake!'

So there's no escaping it, thought the dog. He wiped his muzzle and rose to his feet. I'll have to teach in the school one more day, he thought. Better to spend a few hours teaching children than four months in jail!

(Because the dog had committed two crimes now. Not only had he broken into the school, he had pretended to be a teacher. False

82

pretences, that was what the dog thought the crime was called.)

So he ran all the way to school with the landlord's daughters. And even though he put on a tremendous final spurt, Carmen Ann and Lolita Jane were three lengths ahead of him at the school gates. Three dog's lengths. The bear was standing at the gates with a letter in his paw.

'Take a look at this, my dear colleague,' said the bear. 'The Education Authority is out of its tiny mind!' And he held the letter under the dog's nose.

The dog read: ' . . . afraid we shall be unable to send you a temporary teacher for another three weeks . . . '

'No communication between departments at all!' said the bear. 'Sending me a teacher and then writing to say they can't send one!'

The dog was glad the school bell began ringing just then. He could go to his classroom instead of continuing to discuss the letter with the bear.

'We're going to do a composition today,' the dog told the children. 'Those of you who can write will write it, and those who can't write yet will tell it.'

'What's the subject?' asked Desiree Mary.

'Something really exciting,' said the dog. 'What's happened to you recently that was really exciting?'

'The race to school this morning,' said Carmen Ann.

'Buying cherries yesterday!' said Peter Basil.

'What else?' The dog was rather disappointed.

The children said they were afraid nothing else really exciting had ever happened to them. Their lives were rather boring, and there wasn't much going on in the village.

The dog thought. 'Then we'll have to do something really exciting,' he said, 'so that we can do a composition about it afterwards. What do you think would be really exciting?'

'Flying to the moon!' cried one boy.

'I'm afraid they wouldn't take us,' said the dog.

'Catching a bank robber,' suggested another child.

'We're not likely to find one in a hurry,' said the dog.

'Treasure-hunting,' said another child.

'Where?' asked the dog.

'No idea,' said the child.

'Nor have I, I'm afraid,' said the dog.

'Seeing a ghost!' cried yet another child.

'Ooh, yes!' shouted all the children. 'Seeing a ghost would be really, really exciting!'

'Right,' said the dog. 'Let's go and see a ghost. Luckily there happens to be one down in the school cellar.'

The dog led the children out of the classroom. They stole down to the cellar on tiptoe. When all the children were down there, the dog turned the light out, because you can only talk to ghosts in the pitch dark.

'Please forgive us for disturbing your day's rest, Ghost,' growled the dog into the pitch darkness.

Then he whined softly.

'My pupils here would like to meet you!' he growled.

Then he whined again.

'But if all you do is whine we can't understand you!' he growled.

'Sorry,' said the dog in his high, whining voice, 'but I'm so lonely I've got out of the habit of talking!'

'Why do you stay down in this cellar?' growled the dog. 'Come up to our classroom and then you'll have company!'

'Ghosts can't stand daylight!' whined the dog.

'What sort of a ghost are you anyway?' growled the dog.

'I'm afraid I've forgotten,' whined the dog.

'Can we lay you?' growled the dog.

'Oh yes, I wish you would!' whined the dog.

'What do we need to do?' growled the dog.

'I'm afraid I've forgotten that too!' whined the dog.

The children listened with bated breath, but the dog was beginning to get bored with this conversation, so he growled, 'Oh, well, if you've forgotten everything then we can't help you, and we might as well go back upstairs. Goodbye, Ghost!'

The children protested. They were sorry for the ghost, and determined to lay it.

Hm, thought the dog, how can you lay a ghost that doesn't exist? As he was thinking the question over, a large fly which had lost its way in the cellar hummed around his floppy ears. The dog, who was an expert fly-catcher, picked it off his ear. When he had the fly in his paw, he got an idea.

'Ghost,' he growled, 'we can't lay you because you're so stupid you've forgotten what curse was put on you. But we'll change your

86

shape. We'll change you into a fat fly. Then you needn't fear the daylight, and you can fly around the whole wide world for ever. Would you like that?'

'That would be great,' whined the dog.

'Then we'll recite the shape-changing spell,' growled the dog, and he recited to the children:

Ghost, ghost, who cannot die
change into a nice fat fly.
Leave this cellar cold and dark
be as merry as a lark.
Feel no sorrow, feel no pain,
see the whole wide world again!

The children repeated this spell after the dog, line by line, and then the dog whined as if the ghost had been laid, and switched the cellar light on again.

'Where's the fly?' asked the children.

The dog showed them his closed right fore-paw.

The children put their ears close to his paw, and they could hear the fly buzzing and humming. They were very pleased.

The dog went back up to the classroom with the children. He stood at the teacher's desk and opened his paw. The fat fly rose in the air, circled the ceiling light three times, and then shot out of the window.

'That was really exciting!' cried the children.

The big ones sat down and wrote a composition called: *How We Turned a Ghost into a Fly*.

The little ones sat on the floor round the dog and told him the story of *The Ghostly Fly*.

Ten children told the dog the story, and all ten swore blind that they had seen the ghost. It was an enormous ghost, they said, extremely fat, and it wobbled like lemon blancmange.

The dog had really intended to make his get-away after school that day, but since he had promised the children who could write to read their compositions, and mark each composition with a big red A, he went back to the inn for a little while, borrowed a red ballpoint pen from the landlord, sat down in his room, read the compositions and marked them all with an A. He didn't correct their mistakes, thinking to himself: I don't want to spoil their lovely compositions with red scribbles!

Then the dog wrote the children a letter.
He wrote:

'Dear children,
You are the best pupils I have ever had, and
I am sure you're the best I ever will have. But
I'm afraid I have to leave you today . . . '

When the dog had reached this point in his
letter he put the ballpoint pen down, saying to
himself: it's wrong to tell children lies about
important things. So he crumpled up the letter
and wrote another one.
He wrote:

'Dear children,
I am not a teacher at all. I'm only an ordinary
travelling dog. Please don't feel cross with
me. It was very nice knowing you.
With love from Dog, who will never forget
you.'

The dog went downstairs to get an envelope
from the landlord for his letter. But the landlord
had run out of envelopes. So the dog went to
the shop.

The saleswoman there gave the dog his envelope free. 'My son Basil is in your class,' she
said. 'He tells me you're a really great teacher!'

When the dog got back to his room with
the envelope, Carmen Ann and Lolita Jane were
sitting on his bed, looking sad.

'We were going to bring you some flowers,'
said Carmen Ann.

'To make it nice and comfortable for you
here,' said Lolita Jane.

'And then we read your letter,' said Carmen
Ann.

'Because it's written to us as well as the others,' said Lolita Jane.

The dog hung his head and stared at the claws of his back feet. He felt dreadfully ashamed.

'We don't mind if you're not a trained teacher,' said Carmen Ann.

'And I bet the other children wouldn't mind either,' said Lolita Jane.

'We love you very, very much,' said Carmen Ann.

The dog was moved. He took his handkerchief out of the big green pouch and blew his nose.

'Stay for a week, at least,' begged Lolita Jane.

'Stay for tomorrow, at least!' begged Carmen Ann.

'OK,' growled the dog, wiping two tears of emotion from his eyes and putting the handkerchief away again. 'But it will really be just for tomorrow!'

The dog could refuse nothing to those who really loved him.

So the dog was a teacher for another ten days, because every day the children begged him to stay another day – just one more day. All the children in his class knew he was not a real teacher. Carmen Ann and Lolita Jane had told them, and they had promised not to tell anyone else. The children kept their word, and they had a lovely time with the dog. They went for an educational outing almost every day. Once they went to the bakery and learned to bake bread and rolls. Once they went to the garden centre and learned to re-pot plants. And they went to the tailor, the cobbler, and a farm-yard. One day they planted trees in the school playground: a tree for every child. Another day they painted the ugly grey walls of the school building sky-blue with big paint-brushes. And the dog taught the children to whistle tunes.

But he didn't forget to teach them reading, writing and arithmetic either.

You can hardly do without arithmetic when you have to work out how much paint you need for a whole school building, and how much yeast you need to raise thirteen kilos of flour, and how much fabric you need to make seven pairs of trousers. And as the children always wrote down what they had been doing, they had plenty of writing practice. And every evening the dog sat down and wrote a story about something that had happened to him, and then the children read it next day.

On the twelfth day the dog was being a teacher, it rained in torrents, so the dog didn't take the children for an educational outing. He stayed in the classroom with them, telling them about the photograph album he had in his head, and all the clouds he had collected there. The children and the dog stood at the classroom windows while the dog talked, because the children wanted to *take photographs in their heads* too. Unfortunately, however, the sky was dark grey all over, and there wasn't a single cloud to be seen. And unfortunately, something quite different *was* to be seen: a car driving up to the school. It stopped outside. A man got out of the car, put up an umbrella and made for the school gates. The man was long and thin and judging by his face, he was half a donkey by birth. Or half a human. Depending on your point of view.

The dog said to the children, in an undertone, 'Maybe that's someone's father come to ask some questions!'

The children shook their heads. They knew the fathers of all the people in their class. And they knew the fathers of the children in the other class. 'He's not from this village,' they said.

Then the children and the dog stood perfectly

still. They stood so still that they could hear the school gates creak as the man walked into the school. They heard his footsteps squeaking along the corridor, and they heard him open the door of the headmaster's office and call, 'Where's the Head?'

'Just coming, just coming!' they heard the bear call. 'What's all the hurry?' And then they heard his steps coming stump, stump, stump out of the other classroom.

The bear went into the headmaster's office.

The children and the dog held their breath.

Quietly, they stole over to the wall with the blackboard on it.

The headmaster's office was the other side of that wall. And the wall itself was only a thin, plaster partition. They could hear what was being said the other side of it as clearly as if they were listening to a radio play.

'What can I do for you?' asked the bear.

'I'm from the Education Authority,' said the man.

'Pleased to meet you,' said the bear.

'We have received,' said the man, 'a letter from your local Parents' Association. They want the new teacher you have here to be appointed permanently as a replacement for his sick colleague.'

'Ah, well,' said the bear, 'I'm right behind them there. The children like him very much. In fact, my new colleague is an excellent teacher!'

'But we never sent you any new teacher at all,' said the man.

The bear laughed heartily. 'Well, you're a joker and no mistake!' he said. 'We've had the new teacher here for two whole weeks. Are you telling me there's an imaginary teacher standing in the room next door?'

'If there's anyone standing there,' said the man, 'he's an impostor. Moreover, according to the Parents' Association's letter, this new teacher is a dog. We have never appointed a single dog as a teacher anywhere in the entire district!'

'You don't say!' said the bear, astonished.

'I do,' said the man. 'You've entrusted your pupils here to a charlatan! This dog will be put in prison. The police have already been notified. And the matter reflects no credit on you, either.'

'Children,' whispered the dog, when he had heard this bit, 'I'll have to get out of here!'

'But not through the school gates,' whispered Carmen Ann. 'The police could be there already!'

'I'll get out through the window,' whispered the dog.

'No, don't!' Peter Basil held the dog back by his tail. 'You'll be seen from the Head's window.'

'We must hide you,' said Lolita Jane.

The only place in the classroom big enough for the dog to hide in was the cupboard. The cupboard had shelves for paints and exercise books, chalk and maps, pots of glue, coloured paper, erasers and crayons.

The dog did not want to get into the cupboard. He thought it was undignified to hide from the half-donkey. But as his knees were knocking together from sheer fright, the children managed to drag him over to the cupboard all the same.

One of the children opened the cupboard door. Two of the children lifted the bottom shelf out, three of the children pushed the dog into the cupboard, four of the children shut the cupboard door, Peter Basil locked the cupboard and put the key in his trouser pocket, and then he said, 'Right, everyone back to their desks!'

No sooner were all the children at their desks than the Education Authority man marched into the classroom with the bear.

'Where's that dog?' asked the Education Authority man.

Carmen Ann stood up, looking innocent as an angel.

'Please,' she said, 'the teacher shot out of the door like greased lightning!'

'I think he had to go to the lavatory,' Peter Basil pointed in that direction. 'He probably had a stomach-ache.'

The Education Authority man strode out of the classroom towards the school lavatories. When he saw the window open from the inside, he scrambled through it, shouting, 'Follow me! He can't have got far!'

There was a large meadow behind the school, and beyond the meadow grew a wood. Someone was standing at the far end of the meadow, just where the trees began.

'Come on, Headmaster!' shouted the man from the Education Authority.

The bear marched into the lavatories. The children pressed in behind him. The bear looked out of the lavatory window. 'Yes?' he said to the man from the Education Authority, in friendly tones.

'What do you mean, yes? Get moving!' yelled the man from the Education Authority, pointing in the direction of the wood. 'Is that the dog?'

The bear narrowed his eyes so as to see better. The figure on the outskirts of the wood had a bright blue hat on its head. Everyone in the village knew that the only person who wore a bright blue hat like that was the old ram who lived by picking mushrooms.

'The rain rather spoils my view,' said the bear, 'but yes, I think it could very well be the dog!'

'Then what are you waiting for?' shouted the man from the Education Authority. He put his umbrella up and started to run. Across the meadow, towards the bright blue hat.

The bear sighed, and clambered up on the window-sill.

'Looks as if I'll have to do a spot of jogging myself,' he murmured. But before climbing out of the window, he told the children, 'And you go back to your classroom and clear the cupboard out, understand?'

'Yes!' shouted the children, scuttling back into the classroom. Peter Basil was going to unlock the cupboard, but the key wasn't in his trouser pocket any more. There was a hole in his pocket, and the key must have fallen through the hole. Desperately, the children searched the floor. In the classroom, the corridor and the lavatories. But because they were so excited and kept getting in each other's way, they couldn't find the key.

'This is no good,' said Lolita Jane. 'We'll have to move the whole cupboard.'

Cautiously, the children tipped the cupboard over. Seven children took hold of its right side and seven took hold of its left side. Three children held the bottom of the cupboard and three held the top of the cupboard. The cupboard was rather heavy, but twenty children together are strong if there's something they really want to do.

The children carried the cupboard out of the school building.

'Now where?' panted Peter Basil.

'Home to us,' gasped Carmen Ann and Lolita Jane. 'He'll be safe there!'

They carried the cupboard through the pouring rain to the inn. The few people they met were not surprised to see them. They thought it was just another educational outing. The children were wet through by the time they put the cupboard down in the big room of the inn.

'What on earth have you got there?' asked the landlord.

'The dog!' whispered Carmen Ann into her father's right ear. 'He's not a real teacher!'

'And the Education Authority is after him,' Lolita Jane whispered in her father's left ear.

The landlord nodded. 'I see,' he said. 'So you're giving me this cupboard to store all the old junk I keep in the shed! Very kind of you, children! You can take it to the shed straight away. I'll show you the way.'

The landlord took the children to the shed, where they stood the cupboard on end again. The landlord found a chisel and broke it open.

The dog was a sorry sight! His coat had red, yellow and blue patches all over it, and it was gummed up with glue. The jars of paint and pots of glue had spilled their contents on the way.

Groaning, the dog clambered out. There was blotting paper sticking to his paws, there were pieces of chalk sticking in his tail, bits of maps flapping from his ears, crayons dangled from the fur around his stomach, and erasers clung to his nose like warts.

'He must get under the shower,' said the landlord, 'or that stuff will congeal.' And he told the children, 'Back to school, and hurry!'

The children wanted to stay with the dog. They wanted to wash him, and blow his coat dry, and comfort him. But the landlord chased them away. 'Don't be silly,' he said. 'If the man from the Education Authority realizes you're here, he'll guess the dog can't be far away.'

The children saw the point of that. They went back to school and were sitting at their desks, looking as if butter wouldn't melt in their mouths, before the bear and the man from the Education Authority got back from the wood.

The landlord put the dog under the shower until he was clean. The landlady blew his coat dry with her hair dryer. The landlord wrapped the dog in a bath towel. The landlady washed his clothes. The landlord brought the dog a sandwich. The landlady brought him a cup of beef tea. The landlord said, 'I'm really very sorry, Dog. We all like you here!'

'Aren't you angry with me?' asked the dog, shyly. 'For not being a trained teacher?'

'Who cares?' said the landlady. 'It's not just training that counts. You've got natural talent!'

'But the authorities don't understand that kind of thing,' said the landlord.

Then the landlord and his wife took the dog to their bedroom. He was very tired after all that excitement. He lay down in the double bed, let them cover him, and fell fast asleep.

Around mid-day the policeman came to the inn. 'It's about the teacher,' he said, sighing.

'The one our children like so much.'

'What about him?' asked the landlord.

'There's a warrant out for his arrest,' said the policeman. 'I have to search every house in the village for him.'

'Ours too?' asked the landlady.

'Of course,' said the policeman. 'I'm conducting my search systematically, starting with house Number One. It will take me a good fifteen minutes per house!' And the policeman winked at the landlord and the landlady, and left the inn.

'Seeing ours is number twenty-four . . . ' said the landlord to his wife.

' . . . the dog can sleep a good while longer,' said the landlady to her husband.

Late that afternoon, a tractor drove out of the back yard of the inn. The landlord was driving the tractor. Carmen Ann and Lolita Jane were sitting on the trailer, on top of a huge heap of hay. Just as the policeman came in through the front door of the inn, the tractor drove out of the gate at the back.

The tractor drove a long way out of the village, and stopped at a minor road. The dog crawled out of the hay, along with his fedora, his travelling bag, his case, his big green pouch and his scarf. 'Thanks!' he called to the landlord, and he blew a kiss to the landlord's daughters, and set off along the road. The tractor turned round. Carmen Ann and Lolita Jane, up on the hay, wept bitterly when they saw the dog go off.

The dog marched along the road. He felt like crying himself. He felt lonely and abandoned. He tried to whistle a tune to cheer himself up a bit, but every whistle turned into a sob.

Suddenly he heard the sound of an engine behind him. A car was driving along the road. The dog did not turn round. This is sure to be the policeman, he thought. I'm about to be arrested!

The dog did not even try to hide in the bushes beside the road. He put his luggage down, raised his forepaws in the air, and waited to be arrested.

The car hooted, raced up to the dog, and stopped beside him.

'Climb in!' the bear called through the car window.

The dog put his luggage in the boot and got in beside the bear. The bear accelerated and drove on. The dog thought he was just looking for a good place to turn. However, when they had passed a dozen places which would have been perfect for turning a car, it dawned upon the dog that the bear was not going to take him back to the village and hand him over to the police after all. But he dared not ask where, in that case, the bear was taking him.

The bear drove straight on until the minor road petered out in a small clearing in a wood. He got out and produced a large bundle from the boot.

The bundle was a tent. The bear began to put the tent up. 'We'll stay here until all the fuss has died down,' he said, in tones of satisfaction, 'and then we'll go on again. Is that all right, Dog?'

'We?' asked the dog.

'Well, only if you don't mind my company,' said the bear.

'But don't you have to go back to the school?' said the dog.

The bear shook his head. 'I've been provisionally suspended,' he said. 'For being short-sighted. Because I can't tell a ram from a dog. And for carelessness. Because I don't know what's become of the classroom cupboard. All that will have to be cleared up before I go back, and the Education Authority moves slowly. And I'd have been retiring in six months anyway. And life is too much fun for me to sit about doing nothing until a bunch of nitwits have cleared up some kind of muddle!'

'My own feelings exactly,' said the dog, and he helped the bear put up the tent. The bear started singing a merry song, and the dog whistled an accompaniment. And not one note he whistled turned into a sob.

This story is by Christine Nostlinger.

The One That Got Away

'And what have we to remember to bring tomorrow?' Mrs Cooper asked, at half past three. Malcolm, sitting near the back, wondered why she said 'we'. *She* wasn't going to bring anything.

'Something interesting, Mrs Cooper,' said everyone else, all together.

'And what are we going to do then?'

'Stand up and talk about it, Mrs Cooper.'

'So don't forget. All right. Chairs on tables. Goodbye, Class Four.'

'Goodbye, Mrs Cooper. Goodbye, everybody.'

It all came out ever so slow, like saying prayers in assembly. 'Amen,' said Malcolm, very quietly. Class Four put its chairs on the tables, collected its coats and went home, talking about all the interesting things it would bring into school tomorrow.

Malcolm walked by himself. Mrs Cooper had first told them to find something interesting on Monday. Now it was Thursday and still he had not come up with any bright ideas. There were plenty of things that he found interesting, but the trouble was, they never seemed to interest anyone else. Last time this had happened he had brought along his favourite stone and shown it to the class.

'Very nice, Malcolm,' Mrs Cooper had said. 'Now tell us what's interesting about it.' He hadn't known what to say. Surely anyone looking at the stone could see how interesting it was.

Mary was going to bring her gerbil. James, Sarah and William had loudly discussed rare shells and fossils, and the only spider in the world with five legs.

'It can't be a spider then,' said David, who was eavesdropping.

'It had an accident,' William said.

Isobel intended to bring her pocket calculator and show them how it could write her name by punching in 738051 and turning it upside down. She did this every time, but it still looked interesting.

108

Malcolm could think of nothing.

When he reached home he went up to his bedroom and looked at the shelf where he kept important things: his twig that looked like a stick insect, his marble that looked like a glass eye, the penny with a hole in it and the Siamese-twin jelly-babies, one red, one green and stuck together, back to back. He noticed that they were now stuck to the shelf, too. His stone had once been there as well, but after Class Four had said it was boring he had put it back in the garden. He still went to see it sometimes.

What he really needed was something that could move about, like Mary's gerbil or William's five-legged spider. He sat down on his bed and began to think.

On Friday, after assembly, Class Four began to be interesting. Mary kicked off with the gerbil that whirred round its cage like a hairy balloon with the air escaping. Then they saw William's lame spider. James's fossil, Jason's collection of snail shells stuck one on top of the other like the leaning tower of Pisa, and David's bottled conkers that he had kept in an air-tight jar for three years. They were still as glossy as new shoes.

Then it was Malcolm's turn. He went up

to the front and held out a matchbox. He had
chosen it very carefully. It was the kind with
the same label top and bottom so that when you
opened it you could never be sure that it was
the right way up and all the matches fell out.
Malcolm opened it upside down and jumped.
Mrs Cooper jumped too. Malcolm threw himself down on hands and knees and looked under
her desk.

'What's the matter?' Mrs Cooper said.

'It's fallen out!' Malcolm cried.

'What is it?' Mrs Cooper said, edging away.

'I don't know – it's got six legs and sharp
knees . . . and sort of frilly ginger eyebrows
on stalks —' He pounced. 'There it goes.'

'Where?'

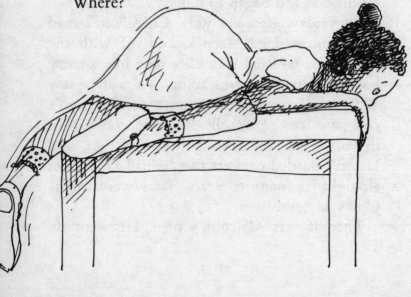

'Missed it,' said Malcolm. 'It's running under your chair, Mary.'

Mary squeaked and climbed on to the table because she thought that was the right way to behave when creepy-crawlies were about.

'I see it!' Jason yelled, and jumped up and down. David threw a book in the direction that Jason was pointing and James began beating the floor with a rolled-up comic.

'I got it – I killed it,' he shouted.

'It's crawling up the curtains,' Sarah said and Mrs Cooper, who was standing by the curtains, moved rapidly away from them.

'It's over by the door,' Mary shrieked, and several people ran to head it off. Chairs were overturned.

Malcolm stood by Mrs Cooper's desk with his matchbox. His contribution was definitely the most interesting thing that anyone had seen that morning. He was only sorry that he hadn't seen it himself.

This story is by Jan Mark.

Broomsticks and Sardines

'Oh bother,' said Mrs Armitage, looking over her coffee-cup at the little heap of sixpences on the sideboard, 'the children have forgotten to take their lunch money to school. You could go that way to the office and leave it, couldn't you, darling?'

The house still reverberated to the slam of the front door, but the children were out of sight, as Mr Armitage gloomily ascertained.

'I hate going to that place,' he said. 'Miss Croot makes me feel so small, and all the little tots look at me.'

'Nonsense, dear. And anyway, why shouldn't they?' Mrs Armitage returned in a marked manner to the *Stitchwoman and Home Beautifier's Journal*, so her husband, with the sigh of a martyr, put on his hat, tucked *The*

113

Times and his umbrella under his arm, and picked up the money. He dropped a kiss on his wife's brow, and in his turn went out, but without slamming the door, into the October day. Instead of going down the cobbled hill towards his office, he turned up the little passageway which led to Miss Croot's kindergarten, which Mark and Harriet attended. It was a small studio building standing beside a large garden which lay behind the Armitage garden; Harriet and Mark often wished that they could go to school by climbing over the fence. Fortunately the children were not allowed to play in the studio garden or, as the Armitage parents often said to each other, shuddering, they would hear the children's voices all day long instead of only morning and evening.

Mr Armitage tapped on the studio door but nobody answered his knock. There was a dead hush inside, and he mentally took his hat off to Miss Croot for her disciplinary powers. Becoming impatient at length, however, he went in, through the lobby where the boots and raincoats lived. The inner door was closed, and when he opened it he stood still in astonishment.

The studio room was quite small, but the little pink and blue and green desks had been

114

shoved back against the walls to make more space. The children were all sitting cross-legged on the floor, quiet as mice, in a ring round the old-fashioned green porcelain stove with its black chimney-pipe which stood on a kind of iron step in the middle of the room. There was a jam cauldron simmering on this stove, and Miss Croot, an exceedingly tall lady with teeth like fence-posts and a great many bangles, was stirring the cauldron and dropping in all sorts of odds and ends.

Mr Armitage distinctly heard her recite:

Eye of newt and toe of frog —

and then he said: 'Ahem,' and, stepping forward, gave her the little stack of warm sixpences which he had been holding in his hand all this time.

'My children forgot their lunch money,' he remarked.

'Oh, thank you, Mr Er,' Miss Croot gratefully if absently replied. '*How* kind. I do like to get it on Mondays. Now a pinch of vervain, Pamela, from the tin on my desk, please.'

A smug little girl with a fringe brought her the pinch.

115

'I hope, ma'am, that *that* isn't the children's lunch,' said Mr Armitage, gazing distastefully into the brew. He saw his own children looking at him pityingly from the other side of the circle, plainly hoping that he wasn't going to disgrace them.

'Oh dear, no,' replied Miss Croot vaguely. 'This is just our usual transformation mixture. There, it's just going to boil.' She dropped in one of the sixpences, and it instantly became a pink moth and fluttered across to the window.

'Well, I must be on my way,' muttered Mr Armitage. 'Close in here, isn't it.'

He stepped carefully back through the seated children to the doorway, noticing as he did so some very odd-looking maps on the walls, a tray of sand marked in hexagons and pentagons, a stack of miniature broomsticks, coloured beads arranged on the floor in concentric circles, and a lot of little plasticine dolls, very realistically made.

At intervals throughout the day Mr Armitage thought rather uneasily about Miss Croot's kindergarten, and when he was drinking his sherry that evening he mentioned the matter to his wife.

'Where are the children now, by the way?' he said.

'In the garden sweeping leaves with their brooms. They made the brooms themselves, with raffia.'

In fact he could see Mark and Harriet hopping about in the autumn dusk. They had become bored with sweeping and were riding on the brooms like horses. As he watched, Mark shouted 'Abracadabra' and his broomstick lifted itself rather jerkily into the air, carried him a few yards, and then turned over, throwing him into the dahlias.

'Oh, jolly good,' exclaimed Harriet. 'Are you hurt? Watch me now.' Her broomstick carried her into the fuchsia bush, where it stuck, and she had some trouble getting down.

'You see what I mean?' said Mr Armitage to his wife.

'Well, I shouldn't worry about it too much,' she answered comfortably, picking up her tatting. 'I think it's much better for them to get that sort of thing out of their systems when they're small. And then Miss Croot is such a near neighbour; we don't want to offend her. Just think how tiresome it was when the Bradmans lived there and kept dropping all their snails over the fence. At least the children play quietly and keep themselves amused nowadays, and that's *such* a blessing.'

Next evening, however, the children were being far from quiet.

Mr Armitage, in his study, could hear raucous shouts and recriminations going on between Mark and Harriet and the Shepherd children, ancient enemies of theirs in the garden on the other side.

'Sucks to you!'

'Double sucks, with brass knobs on.'

'This is a magic wand, I've turned you into a — '

'*Will* you stop that hideous row,' exclaimed Mr Armitage, bursting out of his French window. A deathly hush fell in the garden. He realized almost at once, though, that the silence was due not so much to his intervention as to the fact that where little Richard, Geoffrey and Moira Shepherd had been, there were now three sheep, which Harriet and Mark were regarding with triumphant satisfaction.

'Did you do that?' said Mr Armitage sharply to his children.

'Well – yes.'

'Change them back at once.'

119

'We don't know how.'

'Geoffrey – Moira – your mother says it's bedtime.' Mr Shepherd came out of his greenhouse with a pair of secateurs.

'I say, Shepherd, I'm terribly sorry – my children have changed yours into sheep. And now they say they don't know how to change them back.'

'Oh, don't apologize, old chap. As a matter of fact I think it's a pretty good show. Some peace and quiet will be a wonderful change, and I shan't have to mow the lawn.' He shouted indoors with the liveliest pleasure.

'I say, Minnie! Our kids have been turned into sheep, so you won't have to put them to bed. Dig out a long frock and we'll go to the Harvest Ball.'

A shriek of delight greeted his words.

'All the same, it was a disgraceful thing to do,' said Mr Armitage severely, escorting his children indoors. 'How long will it last?'

'Oh, only till midnight – like Cinderella's coach, you know,' replied Harriet carelessly.

'It would be rather fun if *we* went to the Harvest Ball,' remarked Mr Armitage, in whom the sight of the carefree Shepherd parents had awakened unaccustomed longings.

'Agnes could look after the children, couldn't she?'

'Yes, but I've nothing fit to wear!' exclaimed his wife. 'Why didn't you think of it sooner?'

'Well, dash it all, can't the kids fix you up with something? Not that I approve of this business, in fact I'm going to put a stop to it, but in the meantime — '

Harriet and Mark were delighted to oblige and soon provided their mother with a very palatial crinoline of silver lamé.

'Doesn't look very warm,' commented her husband, 'remember the Assembly Rooms are always as cold as the tomb. Better wear something woolly underneath.'

Mrs Armitage created a sensation at the ball, and was so sought-after that her husband hardly saw her the whole evening. All of a sudden, as he was enjoying a quiet game of whist with the McAlisters, a terrible thought struck him.

'What's the time, Charles?'

'Just on twelve, old man. Time we were toddling. I say, what's up?'

Mr Armitage had fled from the table and was frantically searching the ballroom for his wife. At last he saw her, right across on the other side.

121

'Mary!' he shouted. 'You must come home at once.'

'Why? What? Is it the children — ?' She was threading her way towards him when the clock began to strike. Mr Armitage started and shut his eyes. A roar of applause broke out, and he opened them again to see his wife looking down at herself in bewilderment. She was wearing a scarlet ski-suit. Everyone was crowding round her, patting her on the back and saying that it was the neatest trick they'd seen since the pantomime and how had she done it? She was given a prize of a hundred cigarettes and a bridge marker.

'I had the ski-suit on underneath,' she explained on the way home. 'So as to keep warm, you see. There was plenty of room for it under the crinoline. And what a mercy I did — '

'All this has got to stop,' pronounced Mr Armitage next morning. 'It's Guy Fawkes in a couple of weeks, and can't you just imagine what it'll be like – children flying around on broomsticks and being hit by rockets, outsize fireworks made by fancy methods that I'd rather not go into – it just won't do, I tell you.'

Je crois que vous faites une montagne d'une colline – une colline de — '

'*Une taupinière*,' supplied Harriet kindly. 'And you can call father "*tu*", you know.'

Mark looked sulkily into his porridge and said, 'Well, we've got to learn what Miss Croot teaches us, haven't we?'

'I shall go round and have a word with Miss Croot.'

But as a result of his word with Miss Croot, from which Mr Armitage emerged red and flustered, while she remained imperturbably calm and gracious, such very large snails began to march in an endless procession over the fence from Miss Croot's garden into the Armitage rose-bed, that Mrs Armitage felt obliged to go round to the school and smooth things over.

'My husband always says a great deal more than he means, you know,' she apologized.

'Not at all,' replied Miss Croot affably. 'As a matter of fact I am closing down at Christmas in any case, for I have had a most flattering offer to go as instructress to the young king of Siam.'

'Thank goodness for *that*,' remarked Mr Armitage. 'I should think she'd do well there. But it's a long time till Christmas.'

'At any rate the snails have stopped coming,' said his wife placidly.

Mr Armitage issued an edict to the children.

'I can't control what you do in school, of course, but understand that if there are any more of these tricks outside school there will be *no* Christmas tree, *no* Christmas party, *no* stockings, and *no* pantomime.'

'Yes, we understand,' said Harriet sadly.

Mrs Armitage, too, looked rather sad. She had been thinking what a help the children's gifts would be over the shopping; not perhaps with clothes, as nobody wanted a wardrobe that vanished at midnight, but food! Still, would there be very much nourishment in a joint of mutton that abandoned its eaters in the middle of the night? Probably not; it was all for the best.

Mark and Harriet faithfully, if crossly, obeyed their father's edict and there were no further transformations in the Armitage family circle. But the ban did not, of course, apply to the little Shepherds. Richard, Geoffrey and Moira were not very intelligent children, and it had taken some time for Miss Croot's teaching to sink into them, but when it did they were naturally anxious to retaliate for having been turned into sheep. Mark and Harriet hardly ever succeeded in reaching school in their own shape;

but whether they arrived as ravens, moths, spiders, frogs or pterodactyls, Miss Croot always changed them back again with sarcastic politeness. Everyone became very bored with the little Shepherds and their unchanging joke.

Guy Fawkes came and went with no serious casualties, however, except for a few broken arms and legs and cases of concussion among the children of the neighbourhood, and Mrs Armitage began making plans for her Christmas Party.

'We'll let the children stay up really late this year, shall we?' she said. 'You must admit they've been very good. And you'll dress up as Father Christmas, won't you?'

Her husband groaned, but said that he would.

'I've had such a bright idea. We'll have the children playing Sardines in the dark; they always love that; then you can put on your costume and sack of toys and get into the hiding-place with them, and gradually reveal who you are. Don't you think that's clever?'

Mr Armitage groaned again. He was always sceptical about his wife's good ideas, and this one seemed to him particularly open to mischance. But she looked so pleading that he finally agreed.

'I must make a list of people to ask,' she went on. 'The Shepherds, and the McAlisters, and their children, and Miss Croot, of course — '

'*How* I wish we'd never heard of that woman's school,' said her husband crossly.

Miss Croot was delighted when Mark and Harriet gave her the invitation.

'I'll tell you what would be fun, children,' she said brightly. 'At the end of the evening I'll wave my wand and change you all into dear little fairies, and you can give a performance of that Dance of the Silver Bells that you've been practising. Your parents *will* be surprised. And I shall be the Fairy Queen. I'll compose a little poem for the occasion:

'Now, dear parents, you shall see
What your girls and boys can be,
Lo, my magic wand I raise
And change them into elves and fays . . .

or something along those lines.'

And she retired to her desk in the throes of composition, leaving the children to get on with copying their runes on their own.

'I think she's got a cheek,' whispered Mark indignantly. 'After all, it's our party, not hers.'

'Never mind, it won't take long,' said

126

Harriet, who was rather fond of the Dance of the Silver Bells and secretly relished the thought of herself as a fairy.

The party went with a swing; from the first game of Hunt the Slipper, the first carol, the first sight of Mrs Armitage's wonderful supper with all her specialities, the turkey *vol-au-vent* and Arabian fruit salad.

'Now how about a game of Sardines?' Mrs Armitage called out, finding with astonishment that it was half-past eleven and that none of her guests could eat another crumb.

The lights were turned out.

'Please, we'd rather not play this game. We're a bit nervous,' twittered the Shepherd children, approaching their hostess. She looked at them crossly – really they *were* faddy children.

'Very well, you sit by the fire here till it's time for the Tree.' As she left them she noticed that they seemed to be drawing pictures in the ashes with their fingers, messy little beasts.

She went to help her husband into his cloak and beard.

'Everyone is in the cupboard under the stairs,' she said. 'Harriet hid first, and I told her to go there. I should give them another minute.'

'Who's that wandering about upstairs?'

127

'Oh, that's Miss Croot. Her bun came down, and she went up to fix it. Don't wait for her – there you are, you're done. Off with you.'

Father Christmas shouldered his sack and went along to the stair-cupboard.

'Well,' he exclaimed, in as jovial a whisper as he could manage, stepping into the thick and dusty dark, 'I bet you can't guess who's come in this time?' Gosh, I do feel a fool, he thought.

Silence greeted his words.

'Is there anybody here?' he asked in surprise, and began feeling about in the blackness.

Mrs Armitage, standing by the main switch, was disconcerted to hear shriek upon shriek coming from the cupboard. She threw on the light and her husband came reeling out, his beard awry, parcels falling from his sack in all directions.

'Fish!' he gasped. 'The whole cupboard's full of great wriggling fish.'

It was at this moment that Miss Croot appeared in full fig as the Fairy Queen, and began to recite:

Now, dear parents, you shall see
What your girls and boys can be —

A somewhat shamefaced procession of large silver fish appeared from the cupboard and began wriggling about on their tails.

'Oh dear,' said Miss Croot, taken aback. 'This wasn't what I — '

'D.T.'s,' moaned Mr Armitage. 'I've got D.T.'s.' Then his gaze became fixed on Miss Croot in her regalia, and he roared at her.

'Did you do this, woman? Then out of my house you go, neck and crop.'

'Mr Armitage!' exclaimed Miss Croot, drawing herself up, stiff with rage, and she would certainly have turned him into a toad, had not an interruption come from the little Shepherds, who danced round them in a ring, chanting,

'Tee hee, it was us, it was us! Sucks to the Armitages!'

Luckily at that moment the clock struck twelve, the fish changed back into human form, and by a rapid circulation of fruit-cup, cherry ciderette, and the rescued parcels, Mrs Armitage was able to avert disaster.

'Well, dear friends, I shall say goodbye to you now,' fluted Miss Croot, after ten minutes or so.

'Thank goodness,' muttered Mr Armitage.

'I am off to my new post in Siam, but I shall often think with regret of the little charges left behind, and I hope, dears, that you will all keep up the accomplishments that you have learned from me.' ('They'd better not,' growled her host.) 'And that *you*, pets,' (here she bent a severe look at the little Shepherds) 'will learn some better manners. *Au revoir* to all, and *joyeux Noël.*'

At these words, the carpet beneath her feet suddenly rose and floated her out of the window.

'My carpet!' cried Mr Armitage. 'My beautiful Persian carpet!'

But then they saw that the (admittedly worn) Persian carpet had been replaced by a priceless Aubusson which, unlike Miss Croot's other gifts, did not vanish away at midnight.

All the same, it took Mr Armitage a long time to get used to it. He hated new furniture.

This story is by Joan Aiken.

A is for Aaargh!

'This is Miss Snitchell,' said the headmistress to Class Three. 'She will be taking you while your own teacher is off ill.' She turned to Miss Snitchell and whispered, 'I'm afraid this is the worst class in the school.'

'Don't worry,' whispered Miss Snitchell, 'I know how to deal with rascals.'

The headmistress left and 'Beasty' Barrett, the class bully, grinned and nudged his nasty pal, 'Biff' Higson. 'Let's have some fun with this one,' he whispered. The others heard this and giggled. This could be fun, they thought!

Miss Snitchell cleared her throat. 'Now, children,' she began . . . 'we'll start with an alphabet exercise to test your vocabulary.'

Beasty turned to Biff and winked. 'She thinks we're babies,' he said. 'She's a push-over!'

131

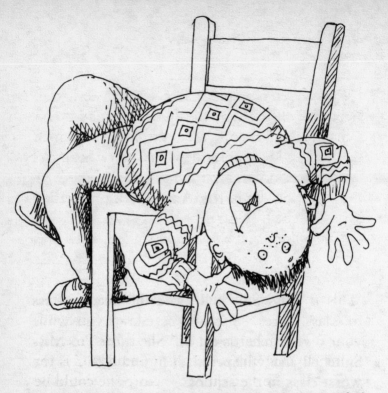

'Who will give me an example to begin with?' said Miss Snitchell, looking round brightly. 'A is for . . . ?'

'AAAAAAARGH!' gurgled Beasty, falling backwards.

The class roared with laughter. Beasty was up to his tricks again! Miss Snitchell smiled faintly. She could take a joke.

'Remove your arrow, boy, and put it away,' she said when the laughter subsided. Miss Snitchell looked around and continued. 'B is for . . . ?' she said.

Beasty set his spider free on the desk-top. Everyone shrieked as the spider scuttled down a chair leg and set off across the floor, but much to Beasty's disappointment his hairy little pet disappeared down a crack in the floorboards.

'Now, sit down and pay attention,' called Miss Snitchell, 'please!'

The children sat down and smiled. This was good fun! When everything was quiet Miss Snitchell began again.

'Boo!' yelled Biff, jumping up from his seat.

'Sit down, child!' said Miss Snitchell sternly. Biff sat down, grinning smugly. Miss Snitchell shook her finger at him and carried on. 'C is for centipede,' she said quickly before she could be interrupted.

'That's right, Miss,' shouted Beasty, 'C is for centipede . . . which is a creepy-crawly like my pet spider!'

'D is for deplorable,' said Miss Snitchell sharply, pointing at Beasty, 'which is what your behaviour has been, young man!' Beasty smiled angelically. The class tittered. 'Now,' smiled Miss Snitchell, the class quiet once more, 'we will continue.'

'E is for . . . EEEEEK!' she shrieked as a mouse ran along the floor and jumped on to one of her shoes. Biff Higson, amid screams of laughter from the class, ran over and picked it up.

'Sorry, Miss,' he said, grinning, as he put it in his pocket. 'It's my pet mouse, Mickey. He escaped.'

Miss Snitchell rapped on the desk for silence. She looked quite stern. 'F is for fright, which is what I got from your pet mouse, my boy.' The class laughed. Miss Snitchell continued. 'G is for grandmother, which is what I am. I have two handsome grandsons, about your age. They are the top goalscorers with their school team. Here is a picture of them holding the Schools Championship Cup.'

The boys were impressed and the girls smiled. But Biff glowered at Beasty. 'She's better than I thought,' he muttered.

'Just wait,' hissed Beasty, 'we haven't finished with her yet!'

'Now,' said Miss Snitchell, 'back to the alphabet. H is for?'

'Handsome,' said good-looking Jim Peters from the back. The other boys rolled their eyes and the girls smiled.

'Good,' said Miss Snitchell.

'H is for horror!' grinned Beasty. 'I love horror films!'

'Do you, now?' said Miss Snitchell. 'Do you really . . . ?' She trailed off and looked at Beasty in an odd way. Beasty grinned and nodded his head.

Miss Snitchell continued. 'I is for . . . ?'

'ICKYPOO!' sniggered Biff loudly. The class giggled.

'That's enough!' snapped Miss Snitchell. 'J is for jungle and jack-in-the-box and juggernaut. K is for . . . ?'

'KING KONG!' bellowed Beasty, lumbering down the aisle like an ape. The class laughed again, encouraging Beasty and Biff.

'L is for Leopard–Man!' snarled Biff, growling and clawing at the girls. 'And M is for Monster movies!'

135

'Yeah . . . M is for Mummy!' shouted Beasty, winding a scarf round his face. 'The Mummy from the Tomb!' he wailed, walking about stiffly.

'N is for nasty!' yelled Biff, throwing his book in the air.

The class was now in uproar. Miss Snitchell shouted but her voice couldn't be heard.

'O is for 'orrible! Like what I am!' yelled Beasty gleefully, jumping on top of a desk. From there he controlled the class just like the conductor of an orchestra. He raised his hand. 'P is for . . . ?'

'PUTRID!' yelled the class.

'Q is for . . . ?'

'QUICKSAND!' they shouted.

'R is for . . . ?'

'ROTTEN!'

'S is for . . . ?'

'SLIME!'

'T is for . . . ?'

'TERRIFIED!'

Miss Snitchell seemed to give up. She slumped forward on her desk. The class looked at her curiously, with evil little grins. They wanted Miss Snitchell to watch them. It would be no fun if she didn't. They were so enjoying themselves! A muffled sound came from the teacher's desk.

'Heh, heh, she's cracked!' grinned Beasty.

They gathered round her desk and listened to Miss Snitchell as she spoke into her arms. 'U is for . . . ' she whispered.

'Louder, Miss!' they shouted gleefully. 'We can't hear you, Miss!' They listened again.

'U . . . ' said Miss Snitchell, her voice slightly muffled by her arms, 'is for . . . UUUUUUUURRGH!'

The class were startled. Uuuurrgh? Was that a word? Puzzled, they looked at each other. Miss Snitchell was going on, her voice growing stronger and louder.

'V is for VAMPIRE!'

The class looked at one another.

'Ha, ha,' said Beasty, 'Miss Snitchell got the joke!'

The class started to laugh but stopped suddenly as Miss Snitchell raised her head.

'W,' she said, 'is for WEREWOLF!!'

The class gasped – the game was definitely over.

Miss Snitchell had changed. Her little bird-like face was hairy and had a pointed nose, ears and dripping fangs . . .

Miss Snitchell *was* a Werewolf! Couldn't she take a joke?

But Miss Snitchell didn't look at all in the mood for laughs. She rose slowly, her red eyes blazing. 'X is for my signature,' she hissed, and scratched a big X on the blackboard with one of her long, sharp, black nails. SCREEEEEEEEEEEEK!! The class moaned.

Miss Snitchell's eyes narrowed. 'Y is for Yeti,' she snarled, holding up a snapshot. 'My hairy monster friend from the Himalayas.'

The class stared open-mouthed, goggle-eyed. Beasty and Biff turned a lovely shade of green as Miss Snitchell's hairy finger pointed at them, and then to the rest of the class.

'And finally,' she growled, 'Z is for Zombie! And all of you will be as watchful as zombies when I teach you from now on. Do you understand?'

The class gulped and nodded together. They understood.

'Now,' said Miss Snitchell, 'as you all seem to be fond of monsters and horror stories, each of you can write out an alphabet for me for tomorrow morning . . . a HORRIBLE alphabet, starting with A is for Aaargh!'

She grinned wickedly at Biff and Beasty who slid down in their seats. The interval bell rang but nobody moved. Miss Snitchell lifted up her hairy snout and gave a long, piercing, triumphant howl.

Just then the headmistress came in.

The class looked at the headmistress.

The headmistress looked at Miss Snitchell, then at the class.

Miss Snitchell smiled sweetly.

'I'm pleased to see that Class Three behaved themselves, Miss Snitchell,' she said.

'Oh, yes,' said Miss Snitchell, 'they were little angels.' She turned to the class and her eyes twinkled mischievously.

'Class dismissed,' she said.

This story is by Frank Rodgers.

Just a Guess

The first thing you noticed about Joe was the colour of his eyes. The table where Philip sat was close to Miss Atkinson's desk, and that morning she brought Joe into the classroom with her and stood him by her while she sat down and got out her register. All the children, boys and girls alike, were staring at the newcomer, some directly, some in a sideways fashion. There were some grins, a giggle or two. Joe looked around the room, and his eyes, Philip noticed, were a brilliant green. Cat's eyes. The bell rang.

'Good morning, children,' said Miss Atkinson.

'Good morning, Miss Atkinson. Good morning all.'

'Answer your names, please.'

Reading the register took long enough for everyone to have a good look at Joe. He was tallish, thinnish, and his clothes were not very smart. His face was very brown, his hair dark, long, a bit greasy. He did not seem embarrassed.

'Now children,' said Miss Atkinson, 'as you can see, Top Class has grown by one this morning. This is Joe Sharp. His family has just come to stay . . . that is, to live . . . in the village. Quite a large family too, I believe. You're the youngest, aren't you, Joe?'

'Yes, Miss.'

'And how many brothers and sisters have you?'

'No sisters, Miss. Just six brothers.'

'A seventh son, are you?' said Miss Atkinson, looking up.

I wonder, she thought, is it possible, could he be the seventh son of a . . .

'Yes, Miss,' said Joe. 'My father is too.'

'Oh,' said Miss Atkinson. 'Yes. Well, now then, let me see.'

She looked round the class. 'Philip. Philip Edwards. You're a sensible person. I want you to look after Joe if you will please. Everything will be strange for him at first. Show him where everything lives. All right?'

'Yes, Miss Atkinson,' Philip said. He saw the green eyes looking at him, and suddenly, for an instant, they shut, both together, in a kind of double wink.

'Now, Joe,' said Miss Atkinson. 'You sit next to Philip, there's room for you there, and I'll get you some exercise books. The rest of you, look at the blackboard please, and get on with the work I've put up there. Later on this morning we have an interesting visitor coming in to school to talk to you – I'll tell you . . . no, I don't think I will. We'll leave it as a surprise.'

She got up and went to the big stock cupboard at the far side of the room.

'Interesting visitor!' whispered Philip across the table.

'Hope it's Gary Lineker!'

'John Barnes,' whispered a boy opposite. 'Gary Lineker is rubbish!'

'Football!' sneered a girl, wrinkling her nose.

'Copper,' said Joe very quietly.

'What?'

'It'll be a copper.'

'How do *you* know?'

'Just a guess.'

'Shhh.'

Miss Atkinson came back with a handful

143

of books, a pencil, a ruler, a rubber.

When the bell went for morning play-time Philip said to the new boy 'Come on then. You'd better come with me. Better put your coat on, it's cold.'

'I haven't got one,' said Joe.

'Oh,' said Philip. He put on his new anorak, blue with a red stripe down each arm and a furry hood. He felt a little awkward. 'Birthday present,' he said.

'November the twenty-third,' said Joe.

'What?' said Philip in amazement.

'Just a guess.'

'How . . . oh, I get it,' said Philip. 'You looked at the register. While Miss Atkinson was talking. You must have sharp eyes.'

'Yes,' said Joe.

In the roaring, screaming, galloping play-ground the two boys stood in a sheltered corner. Philip didn't feel he could dash off to play Bulldog with his particular friends, and the December winds were cold for someone without a top coat, specially somebody as thin as this one. He took a Penguin out of his anorak pocket.

'Have a bit?' he said.

'No thanks,' said Joe. 'Don't want to spoil my appetite for lunch. It's my favourite.'

'What is?'

'Spam fritters and chips.'

Clever Dick, thought Philip, I've got him this time. He hasn't seen the list in the hall. He's just a know-all. It's roast beef.

'Want to bet?' he said.

'I haven't any money,' Joe said.

'Well, I'll tell you what,' Philip said. He put his hand in his trouser pocket. 'I've got this 10p piece, see? If it is Spam fritters and chips for lunch, I'll give it to you, just give it to you. If you're wrong, well, you needn't give me anything.' That's fair, he thought. After all I do actually *know* it's roast beef.

'All right,' said Joe. The green eyes looked straight into Philip's and then shut suddenly, momentarily, in that curious double wink. Philip wanted to smile back, but he felt embarrassed and began to flip the 10p piece in the air, using the pressure of thumb against forefinger, the proper way, the way referees did. He had only lately learned to do this and was proud of it.

Joe stood by him silently, shivering a little in

the cold wind. A gang of younger boys dashed past, and one shouted 'Who's your friend then, Phil?' A group of small girls in woolly hats cantered by, driving each other in harnesses made of skipping ropes. The horses neighed and the drivers cried 'Gee up!' and 'Steady!'

'Heads,' said Joe suddenly. Philip, who had been catching the coin on the back of his left hand and covering it with the fingers of his right, exposed the result of the latest toss. It was a head.

'Try again,' Philip said. He tossed the coin three times and each time Joe called correctly.

'You couldn't get it right ten times running,' said Philip, 'I bet you couldn't. Want to bet?'

'I haven't got any money,' Joe said.

'Oh, it doesn't matter. Just try it.'

Philip tossed his 10p piece ten times. Each time Joe called correctly. Philip scratched his head.

'How d'you do that?' he said.

'Just a guess.'

'You're just lucky, I reckon. Let's try it again.'

'No time,' Joe said. 'It's twenty to eleven. The bell will go any second.'

Philip looked at Joe's thin bare wrists.

'How do you know?' he said. 'You haven't got a watch.'

The bell rang.

As they joined the rush back into school, Philip remembered what Miss Atkinson had said about an interesting visitor. What had Joe said? 'Copper.' I shouldn't be surprised, Philip found himself thinking, and then a funny shiver ran down his spine as they entered the class-room. The curtains were drawn, a screen was set up against one wall, and cables snaked across the floor to a film projector on Miss Atkinson's desk. She stood behind it, and beside her was the uniformed figure of a tall police sergeant.

'Sit down quietly, children,' said Miss Atkinson. Philip forced himself not to look at his neighbour. He didn't want to see that double wink. His mind felt swimmy. Dimly he heard snatches of talk . . . 'Sergeant Harrison . . . Road Safety Division . . . film to show you . . . ', and then a deep voice asking questions . . . 'How . . . When . . . What would you do . . . ?'

Hands were shooting up everywhere, and once he was conscious of Joe's voice answering something.

'Good. Very good indeed,' said the sergeant.

147

'I didn't expect anyone to know that one. How did you know, son?'

'Just a guess.'

Then the projector began to run. It was a good film, an interesting film designed to catch and hold children's attention, and gradually Philip began to concentrate on it. It ended with a simulated road accident, where a boy dashed suddenly across a road, right under the wheels of a double-decker bus. It was very realistic.

The projector fell silent, and the only noise in the classroom was a thin metallic ssswish as Miss Atkinson opened the curtains. The sun had come out, and the audience blinked at the sudden light.

'One last thing,' said Sergeant Harrison in his deep voice.

'One last piece of advice I've got for you lot. You've proved to me this morning that you know quite a bit about the Green Cross Code. You've answered most of my questions pretty well.' He looked at Joe. 'One of them very well. I shouldn't have expected any local lad to have been able to answer that particular one.'

'Joe's new, Sergeant,' said Miss Atkinson. 'It's his first day. His people are travellers – you may have seen their caravans on the common. I expect he's been all over the place, have you Joe?'

'Yes, Miss.'

'Ah, gypsy are you?' said Sergeant Harrison, but he did not say it unkindly, and he smiled as he said it.

'Yes, Sir.'

'Reckon you'll be here long?'

'No, Sir.'

Philip felt a sudden ache.

'Anyway,' said the sergeant. 'As I was saying. Here's one last piece of advice. You all saw how that film finished. Well, don't . . . think . . . it . . . can't . . . happen . . . to . . . you. We all know that was only a mock-up. The boy acting the part didn't get killed, of course. But boys do, and girls, somewhere, every day of every week of every year. So don't think "that couldn't be me". It could. So take care.'

'Paint monitors,' said Miss Atkinson a quarter of an hour later, when the screen and projector had been stowed away, and the tall sergeant had put on his peaked cap and gone. 'Angela. Sue. Judith. Would you please put the tables ready after you've had your lunch. That film should have left us all with lots of pictures in our minds. This afternoon we'll see if we can put them on paper. Now go and wash your hands, everybody, and line up by the hall door.'

Standing beside Joe in the queue, Philip listened to the pair in front.

'What is it today?'

'Roast beef.'

'Ugh!'

'Don't you like it?'

'Not much.'

They all trooped in, and when places had been settled and grace said, Mrs Wood the cook appeared in the doorway of the kitchen.

'I'm sorry, children,' she said, 'there's been a bit of a mix-up. The beef for today's lunch didn't turn up, but I don't think you'll be too disappointed.' She paused.

Philip put his hand in his pocket.

'It's Spam fritters and chips,' she said.

There were one or two 'Oh's', a loud murmur of 'MMM!s'.

'Quiet, please,' said the teacher on dinner duty.

'Keep it,' whispered Joe. 'You keep it.' Philip took his hand out of his pocket. He looked at Joe and got the double wink.

After lunch, in the playground, everybody

knew. Top Class had told the rest, and somehow everyone except the littlest ones managed to pass close to the spot where Philip and Joe were standing. A gypsy! There was giggling. Philip could hear some of the passing comments and they were not kind. 'My dad says they're dirty.' 'They nick things.' 'Horses.' 'Babies.' More giggles. 'They eat hedgehogs.' A snort of laughter.

'Can you tell fortunes, diddakoi?' said Mickey Bean, a big boy who was always looking for trouble and finding it. He stood in front of Joe, quite close, picking his nose with his thumb. Philip felt himself grow suddenly, furiously, angry.

'I can, Mickey,' he said in a choky voice, 'and yours is, you'll get your face smashed in.'

Mickey Bean took his thumb out and clenched his fist.

'Why, you . . . ' he began, but Joe said quietly, 'Pack it in.' He looked at Mickey with his green eyes, and after a moment Mickey looked away.

'Come on, Phil,' said Joe, and they walked off together.

'That was nice of you,' he said, 'sticking up for me.'

They stood side by side at the far end of the

151

playground, their fingers hooked through the wire mesh of the boundary fence, and stared at the traffic going up and down the village street. Philip swallowed.

'Can you?' he said. 'Tell fortunes, I mean?'

'Fortunes?' Joe said. 'I dunno about fortunes. I know what's going to happen. Sometimes. Not always of course.'

'Well, could you . . . ' Philip looked around, ' . . . could you . . . tell what will be the next thing to come round the corner, down there, at the end of the street?'

'Probably,' Joe said. 'Want to bet?' he said, and he gave the double wink, very quickly. The twinkling of an eye, two eyes rather, thought Philip, grinning.

'I haven't got any money,' he said. 'What's in my pocket is yours, really.'

'Well, all right then, if I'm wrong,' said Joe, 'it's yours again.'

'OK,' Philip said. They stared down the street, empty for a moment.

'Private car,' Joe said. '"S" registration. Four-door. Pale blue. Lady driving.' He paused. 'It's a Ford.'

They waited five, ten seconds. Suddenly a car came round the wall of the end house in the street, and drove up towards them, and passed them. It was a four-door 'S' registration saloon with a lady at the wheel. It was pale blue.

'It's a Vauxhall,' Philip said slowly. He looked sideways at Joe.

'Just a guess,' Joe said. 'You have a go,' he said.

Philip tried 'Red car' and got a bicycle, 'Lorry' and got the post van, 'Bus' and round the corner came an old Morris 1000. 'It's Miss Atkinson,' he said as it drew near and began to indicate to turn in to the school road. 'I expect she's been down to Beezer's, she often does at lunch-time.' Beezer's was the village shop which sold everything you could imagine, and Philip was about to explain this to the new boy when it occurred to him that he needn't bother. Joe probably knew exactly what she'd bought. Before he could voice the thought, Joe said, 'All right, if you really want to know – a small brown loaf, six oranges, and a packet of Daz. Oh, and something wrapped in newspaper. Not sure what it is. It's dirty, I think.'

And of course when Miss Atkinson had disappeared into the school, and they wandered down and peeped in the car, there they were on the back seat, bread, fruit, soap–powder, and a head of celery.

Philip's earlier feeling about Joe, a scary feeling that the green eyes could somehow see into the future, had already altered quite a bit. It wasn't a feeling now, it was a certainty, and therefore not as frightening, though just as exciting.

'I suppose you know what I'm going to paint this afternoon,' he said.

'Yes,' Joe said.

At that moment the bell rang for afternoon school. The tables were ready, covered with old newspapers, the paints, brushes, palettes, and mixing dishes put out.

'Painting aprons, everybody, and sleeves rolled tightly, please,' said Miss Atkinson. 'Joe Sharp, I've got an old shirt for you from my odds–and–ends cupboard.'

I know exactly what I'm going to paint, thought Philip. How curious that someone else does too. Before I've even made a mark on the paper.

He began to draw with a pencil, little figures, lots of them, like matchstick men. It was to be a picture of the children coming out of school and crossing the road. With Mrs Maybury the

154

lollipop lady. And lots of cars and buses and lorries and motorbikes. He was so absorbed that it was some time before he realized that Joe's paper was still quite blank.

'What's the matter, Joe?' said Miss Atkinson, coming round.

'Aren't you feeling well?'

'Too many Spam fritters,' someone said, and there was giggling.

'I'm all right, Miss,' Joe said softly.

'Well, come along then. You must make a start. Think about this morning's film. Haven't you got some sort of picture in your mind?'

'Yes, Miss,' Joe said. He picked up a brush and began to put paint on his piece of paper, big splashes of it, with big brush strokes, very quickly. Miss Atkinson went away, and Philip began to colour in his matchstick men, carefully, neatly. He forgot about Joe or indeed anybody else in the room until he heard Miss Atkinson's voice again.

'Why, Joe,' she said, 'that's a strange picture. What's it supposed to be?'

'It's an accident, Miss,' Joe said, and Philip, turning to look, found the green eyes fixed on him with the strangest expression. Quickly Philip looked at Joe's picture. There were no

figures in it, no shapes. There were just splodges
of colour on a background of bluey-black. At
one side there was something that might have
been a tree, or a post perhaps, with a stripey
trunk bent over in the middle, an orange blob
on the end of it. Under that there was a red
squidge, and in the middle of the painting a
kind of chequered path with a big dark mass
on it.

'Yes,' Miss Atkinson said. 'I see.'

'What is it?' Philip whispered when she had

gone away. 'What's the matter? Why are you looking at me like that?'

'It's nothing,' Joe said, and then suddenly, violently, he jumped to his feet, knocking over his chair, and picking up his painting he tore it noisily across, in half, then into quarters, and then again and again till there wasn't a piece bigger than a postage stamp. Everyone stared open-mouthed.

'Joe!' cried Miss Atkinson. 'What in the world . . . ? Look, young man, I don't give out good quality paper and expensive paints so that you can . . . ' She stopped, seeing the curious pallor in the brown face. 'Are you quite sure you're feeling all right?'

'Yes, Miss. Sorry, Miss,' Joe said.

'Well, it's too late to start again now,' Miss Atkinson said. 'Put all those scraps into the wastepaper basket. The rest of you, finish off as soon as you can and start tidying up.'

'Wait for me,' Joe said, when they had been dismissed and were crossing the road with a crowd of others under Mrs Maybury's eagle eye. It was raining and misty and getting dark all at once, and the water ran off the lolli-pop lady's cap and yellow oilskins. There was only one pavement in this part of the street, so everybody crossed before turning their separate ways.

'We can walk down together,' Philip said. 'If your, um, caravan's on the common, I live down that way. Our house is called . . . ' 'I know,' said Joe. 'Of course,' Philip said.

'The only difference is,' he went on, 'that you can stay on this side now, but I cross over the zebra.'

'Between Beezer's and the Post Office,' Joe said.

'Yes.'

'You *mustn't.*'

'What?'

'You mustn't. Whatever you do, you mustn't go on that zebra crossing tonight.'

'Oh, but look,' Philip said, 'I promised Mum I'd always use the crossing. The traffic whizzes along here. And you heard what the policeman said this morning about zebras.'

'You mustn't,' Joe said doggedly, the rain running down his hair and making it look longer and greasier than ever.

'It was that painting of yours, wasn't it?' said Philip. 'You sort of saw something in it, did you?'

Joe nodded.

'Yes, but after all that's just . . . '

'Just a guess,' Joe said.

Philip stopped and looked into the green eyes. They shut, quickly, in the double wink, and Philip grinned.

'Oh, all right,' he said, 'if it makes you any happier I'll cross over earlier.'

They walked on a bit till they came opposite the Post Office, where there was a pavement on each side of the street. Philip looked left, looked right, looked left again, and went carefully over.

They walked on, on opposite sides now, till they came to the zebra crossing, where they stopped and faced one another across the road. It was nearly dark, and the street lights made yellow reflections in the pools of water glistening on the road.

'G'night then, Joe,' Philip called. 'See you in the morning,' but any answer was drowned in a sudden squealing of brakes. The red sports car, travelling fast, tried too suddenly to stop at the sight of two boys, both apparently about to cross. The tyres found no grip on the wet surface and the car skidded wildly sideways, straight at Joe.

Philip heard a crash, as it hit the Belisha beacon, which broke, almost in the middle,

159

so that the top part with its orange ball came slowly down like a flag lowered to half mast.

'He guessed wrong! He guessed wrong! He guessed wrong!' went racing through Philip's brain. He had not seen Joe's wild leap to safety. The car obscured it, and the rain, and the gloom.

'Joe! Joe!' Philip shouted, and he ran madly across the zebra crossing.

He did not see the lorry, and the lorry did not see him. Until the last moment.

Which was too late.

This story is by Dick King-Smith.

Prairie School

Monday morning came. As soon as Laura and Mary had washed the breakfast dishes, they went up the ladder and put on their Sunday dresses. Mary's was a blue-sprigged calico, and Laura's was red-sprigged.

Ma braided their hair very tightly and bound the ends with thread. They could not wear their Sunday hair-ribbons because they might lose them. They put on their sunbonnets, freshly washed and ironed.

Then Ma took them into the bedroom. She knelt down by the box where she kept her best things, and she took out three books. They were the books she had studied when she was a little girl. One was a speller, and one was a reader, and one was a 'rithmetic.

She looked solemnly at Mary and Laura, and they were solemn, too.

'I am giving you these books for your very own, Mary and Laura,' Ma said. 'I know you will take care of them and study them faithfully.'

'Yes, Ma,' they said.

She gave Mary the books to carry. She gave Laura the little tin pail with their lunch in it, under a clean cloth.

'Goodbye,' she said. 'Be good girls.'

Ma and Carrie stood in the doorway, and Jack went with them down the knoll. He was puzzled. They went on across the grass where

the tracks of Pa's wagon wheels went, and Jack
stayed close beside Laura.

When they came to the ford of the creek,
he sat down and whined anxiously. Laura had
to explain to him that he must not come any
farther. She stroked his big head and tried to
smooth out the worried wrinkles. But he sat
watching and frowning while they waded across
the shallow, wide ford.

They waded carefully and did not splash
their clean dresses. A blue heron rose from
the water, flapping away with his long legs
dangling. Laura and Mary stepped carefully on
to the grass. They would not walk in the dusty
wheel tracks until their feet were dry, because
their feet must be clean when they came to
town.

The new house looked small on its knoll with
the great green prairie spreading far around it.
Ma and Carrie had gone inside. Only Jack sat
watching by the ford.

Mary and Laura walked on quietly.

Dew was sparkling on the grass. Meadow
larks were singing. Snipes were walking on
their long, thin legs. Prairie hens were clucking
and tiny prairie chicks were peeping. Rabbits

stood up with paws dangling, long ears twitching, and their round eyes staring at Mary and Laura.

Pa had said that town was only two and a half miles away, and the road would take them to it. They would know they were in town when they came to a house.

Large white clouds sailed in the enormous sky and their grey shadows trailed across the waving prairie grasses. The road always ended a little way ahead, but when they came to that ending, the road was going on. It was only the tracks of Pa's wagon through the grass.

'For pity's sake, Laura,' said Mary, 'keep your sunbonnet on! You'll be brown as an Indian, and what will the town girls think of us?'

'I don't care!' said Laura, loudly and bravely.

'You do, too!' said Mary.

'I don't either!' said Laura.

'You do!'

'I don't!'

'You're just as scared of town as I am.' said Mary.

Laura did not answer. After a while she took hold of her sunbonnet strings and pulled the bonnet up over her head.

164

'Anyway, there's two of us,' Mary said.

They went on and on. After a long time they saw town. It looked like small blocks of wood on the prairie. When the road dipped down, they saw only grasses again and the sky. Then they saw the town again, always larger. Smoke went up from its stovepipes.

The clean, grassy road ended in dust. This dusty road went by a small house and then past a store. The store had a porch with steps going up to it.

Beyond the store there was a blacksmith shop. It stood back from the road, with a bare place in front of it. Inside it a big man in a leather apron made a bellows puff! puff! at red coals. He took a white-hot iron out of the coals with tongs, and swung a big hammer down on it, whang! Dozens of sparks flew out tiny in the daylight.

Beyond the bare place was the back of a building. Mary and Laura walked close to the side of this building. The ground was hard there. There was no more grass to walk on.

In front of this building, another wide, dusty road crossed their road. Mary and Laura stopped. They looked across the dust at the fronts of two more stores. They heard a confused noise of children's voices. Pa's road did not go any farther.

'Come on,' said Mary, low. But she stood still. 'It's the school where we hear the hollering. Pa said we would hear it.'

Laura wanted to turn around and run all the way home.

She and Mary went slowly walking out into the dust and turned towards that noise of voices. They went padding along between two stores. They passed piles of boards and shingles; that must be the lumber-yard where Pa got the boards for the new house. Then they saw the schoolhouse.

It was out on the prairie beyond the end of the dusty road. A long path went towards it through the grass. Boys and girls were in front of it.

Laura went along the path towards them and Mary came behind her. All those girls and boys stopped their noise and looked. Laura kept on going nearer and nearer all those eyes, and suddenly, without meaning to, she swung the dinner-pail and called out, 'You all sounded just like a flock of prairie chickens!'

They were surprised. But they were not as much surprised as Laura. She was ashamed, too.

Mary gasped, 'Laura!' Then a freckled boy with fire-coloured hair yelled. 'Snipes, yourselves! Snipes! Snipes! Long-legged snipes!'

Laura wanted to sink down and hide her legs. Her dress was too short, it was much shorter than the town girls' dresses. So was Mary's. Before they came to Plum Creek, Ma had said they were outgrowing those dresses. Their bare legs did look long and spindly, like snipes' legs.

All the boys were pointing and yelling, 'Snipes! Snipes!'

Then a red-headed girl began pushing those boys and saying: 'Shut up! You make too much noise! Shut up, Sandy!' she said to the red-headed boy, and he shut up. She came close to Laura and said:

'My name is Christy Kennedy, and that horrid boy is my brother Sandy, but he doesn't mean any harm. What's your name?'

Her red hair was braided so tightly that the braids were stiff. Her eyes were dark blue, almost black, and her round cheeks were freckled. Her sunbonnet hung down her back.

'Is that your sister?' she said. 'Those are my sisters.' Some big girls were talking to Mary. 'The big one's Nettie, and the black-

167

haired one's Cassie, and then there's Donald and me and Sandy. How many brothers and sisters have you?'

'Two,' Laura said. 'That's Mary, and Carrie's the baby. She has golden hair, too. And we have a bulldog named Jack. We live on Plum Creek. Where do you live?'

'Does your Pa drive two bay horses with black manes and tails?' Christy asked.

'Yes,' said Laura. 'They are Sam and David, our Christmas horses.'

'He comes by our house, so you came by it, too,' said Christy. 'It's the house before you came to Beadle's store and post-office, before you get to the blacksmith shop. Miss Eva Beadle's our teacher. That's Nellie Oleson.'

Nellie Oleson was very pretty. Her yellow hair hung in long curls, with two big blue ribbon bows on top. Her dress was thin white lawn, with little blue flowers scattered over it, and she wore shoes.

She looked at Laura and she looked at Mary, and she wrinkled up her nose.

'Hm!' she said. 'Country girls!'

Before anyone else could say anything, a bell rang. A young lady stood in the schoolhouse doorway, swinging the bell in her hand. All the boys and girls hurried by her into the schoolhouse.

She was a beautiful young lady. Her brown hair was frizzed in bangs over her brown eyes, and done in thick braids behind. Buttons sparkled all down the front of her bodice, and her skirts were drawn back tightly and fell down behind in big puffs and loops. Her face was sweet and her smile was lovely.

She laid her hand on Laura's shoulder and said, 'You're a new little girl, aren't you?'

'Yes, Ma'am,' said Laura.

'And is this your sister?' Teacher asked, smiling at Mary.

'Yes, Ma'am,' said Mary.

'Then come with me,' said Teacher, 'and I'll write your names in my book.'

169

They went with her the whole length of the schoolhouse, and stepped up on the platform.

The schoolhouse was a room made of new boards. Its ceiling was the underneath of shingles, like the attic ceiling. Long benches stood one behind another down the middle of the room. They were made of planed boards. Each bench had a back, and two shelves stuck out from the back, over the bench behind. Only the front bench did not have any shelves in front of it, and the last bench did not have any back.

There were two glass windows in each side of the schoolhouse. They were open, and so was the door. The wind came in, and the sound of waving grasses, and the smell and the sight of the endless prairie and the great light of the sky.

Laura saw all this while she stood with Mary by Teacher's desk and they told her their names and how old they were. She did not move her head, but her eyes looked around.

A water-pail stood on a bench by the door. A bought broom stood in one corner. On the wall behind Teacher's desk there was a smooth space of boards painted black. Under it was a little trough. Some kind of short, white sticks lay in the trough, and a block of wood with a woolly bit of sheepskin pulled tightly around it and nailed down. Laura wondered what those things were.

Mary showed Teacher how much she could read and spell. But Laura looked at Ma's book and shook her head. She could not read. She was not even sure of all the letters.

'Well, you can begin at the beginning, Laura,' said Teacher, 'and Mary can study farther on. Have you a slate?'

They did not have a slate.

'I will lend you mine,' Teacher said. 'You cannot learn to write without a slate.'

She lifted up the top of her desk and took out the slate. The desk was made like a tall box, with one side cut out for her knees. The top rose up on bought hinges, and under it was the place where she kept things. Her books were there, and the ruler.

Laura did not know until later that the ruler was to punish anyone who fidgeted or whispered in school. Anyone who was so naughty had to walk up to Teacher's desk and hold out her hand while Teacher slapped it many times, hard, with the ruler.

But Laura and Mary never whispered in

school, and they always tried not to fidget. They sat side by side on a bench and studied. Mary's feet rested on the floor, but Laura's dangled. They held their book open on the board shelf before them, Laura studying the front of the book and Mary studying farther on, and the pages between standing straight up.

Laura was a whole class by herself, because she was the only pupil who could not read. Whenever Teacher had time, she called Laura to her desk and helped her read letters. Just before dinnertime that first day, Laura was able to read, C A T, cat. Suddenly she remembered and said, 'P A T, Pat!'

Teacher was surprised.

'R A T, rat!' said Teacher. 'M A T, mat!' and Laura was reading! She could read the whole first row in the speller.

At noon all the other children and Teacher went home to dinner. Laura and Mary took their dinner-pail and sat in the grass against the shady side of the empty schoolhouse. They ate their bread and butter and talked.

'I like school,' Mary said.

'So do I,' said Laura. 'Only it makes my legs tired. But I don't like that Nellie Oleson that called us country girls.'

'We are country girls,' said Mary.

'Yes, and she needn't wrinkle her nose!' Laura said.

Jack was waiting to meet them at the ford that night, and at supper they told Pa and Ma all about school. When they said they were using Teacher's slate, Pa shook his head. They must not be beholden for the loan of a slate.

Next morning he took his money out of the fiddle-box and counted it. He gave Mary a round silver piece to buy a slate.

'There's plenty of fish in the creek,' he said. 'We'll hold out till wheat-harvest.'

'There'll be potatoes pretty soon, too,' said Ma. She tied the money in a handkerchief and pinned it inside Mary's pocket.

Mary clutched that pocket all the way along the prairie road. The wind was blowing. Butterflies and birds were flying over the waving grasses and wild flowers. The rabbits loped before the wind and the great clear sky curved over it all. Laura swung the dinner-pail and hippety-hopped.

In town, they crossed dusty Main Street and climbed the steps to Mr Oleson's store. Pa had said to buy the slate there.

Inside the store there was a long board
counter. The wall behind it was covered with
shelves, full of tin pans and pots and lamps
and lanterns and bolts of coloured cloth. By
the other wall stood ploughs and kegs of nails
and rolls of wire, and on that wall hung saws
and hammers and hatchets and knives.

A large, round, yellow cheese was on the
counter, and on the floor in front of it was a

barrel of molasses, and a whole keg of pickles, and a big wooden box full of crackers, and two tall wooden pails of candy. It was Christmas candy; two big pails full of it.

Suddenly the back door of the store burst open, and Nellie Oleson and her little brother Willie came bouncing in. Nellie's nose wrinkled at Laura and Mary, and Willie yahed at them: 'Yah! Yah! Long-legged snipes!'

'Shut up, Willie,' Mr Oleson said. But Willie did not shut up. He went on saying: 'Snipes! Snipes!'

Nellie flounced by Mary and Laura, and dug her hands into a pail of candy. Willie dug into the other pail. They grabbed all the candy they could hold and stood cramming it into their mouths. They stood in front of Mary and Laura, looking at them, and did not offer them even one piece.

'Nellie! You and Willie go right back out of here!' Mr Oleson said.

They went on stuffing candy into their mouths and staring at Mary and Laura. Mr Oleson took no more notice of them. Mary gave him the money and he gave her the slate. He said: 'You'll want a slate pencil, too. Here it is. One penny.'

Nellie said, 'They haven't got a penny.'

'Well, take it along, and tell your Pa to give me the penny next time he comes to town,' said Mr Oleson.

'No, Sir. Thank you,' Mary said. She turned around and so did Laura, and they walked out of the store. At the door Laura looked back. And Nellie made a face at her. Nellie's tongue was streaked red and green from the candy.

'My goodness!' Mary said, 'I couldn't be as mean as that Nellie Oleson.'

Laura thought: 'I could. I could be meaner to her than she is to us, if Ma and Pa would let me.'

They looked at their slate's smooth, soft-grey surface, and its clean, flat wooden frame, cunningly fitted together at the corners. It was a handsome slate. But they must have a slate pencil.

Pa had already spent so much for the slate that they hated to tell him they must have another penny. They walked along soberly, till suddenly Laura remembered their Christmas pennies. They still had those pennies that they had found in their stockings on Christmas morning in Indian Territory.

Mary had a penny, and Laura had a penny, but they needed only one slate pencil. So they decided that Mary would spend her penny for the pencil and after that she would own half of Laura's penny. Next morning they bought the pencil, but they did not buy it from Mr Oleson. They bought it at Mr Beadle's store and post-office, where Teacher lived, and that morning they walked on to school with Teacher.

All through the long, hot weeks they went to school, and every day they liked it more. They liked reading, writing, and arithmetic. They liked spelling-down on Friday afternoons. And Laura loved recess, when the little girls rushed out into the sun and wind, picking wild flowers among the prairie grasses and playing games.

The boys played boys' games on one side of the schoolhouse; the little girls played on the other side, and Mary sat with the other big girls, ladylike on the steps.

The little girls always played ring-around-a-rosy, because Nellie Oleson said to. They got tired of it, but they always played it, till one day, before Nellie could say anything, Laura said, 'Let's play Uncle John!'

'Let's! Let's!' the girls said, taking hold of

hands. But Nellie grabbed both hands full of Laura's long hair and jerked her flat on the ground.

'No! No!' Nellie shouted. 'I want to play ring-around-a-rosy!'

Laura jumped up and her hand flashed out to slap Nellie. She stopped it just in time. Pa said she must never strike anybody.

'Come on, Laura,' Christy said, taking her hands. Laura's face felt bursting and she could hardly see, but she went circling with the others around Nellie. Nellie tossed her curls and flounced her skirts because she had her way. Then Christy began singing and all the others joined in:

'Uncle John is sick abed.
What shall we send him?'

'No! No! Ring-around-a-rosy!' Nellie screamed. 'Or I won't play!' She broke through the ring and no-one went after her.

'All right, you get in the middle, Maud,' Christy said. They began again.

'Uncle John is sick abed.
What shall we send him?
A piece of pie, a piece of cake,
Apple and dumpling!
What shall we send it in?
A golden saucer.
Who shall we send it by?
The governor's daughter.
If the governor's daughter ain't at home,
Who shall we send it by?'

Then all the girls shouted,

'By Laura Ingalls!'

Laura stepped into the middle of the ring and they danced around her. They went on playing Uncle John till Teacher rang the bell. Nellie was in the schoolhouse, crying, and she said she was so mad that she was never going to speak to Laura or Christy again.

But the next week she asked all the girls to a party at her house on Saturday afternoon. She asked Christy and Laura, specially.

This story is by Laura Ingalls Wilder.

Hey, Danny!

'Right,' said Danny's mother sternly. 'That schoolbag cost ten dollars. You can just save up your pocket money to buy another one. How could you possibly lose a big schoolbag, anyhow?'

'Dunno,' said Danny. 'I just bunged in some empty bottles to take back to the milkbar, and I was sort of swinging it round by the handles coming home, and it sort of fell over that culvert thing down on to a truck on the freeway.'

'And you forgot to write your name and phone number in it as I told you to,' said Mrs Hillerey. 'Well, you'll just have to use my blue weekend bag till you save up enough pocket money to replace the old one. And no arguments!'

Danny went and got the blue bag from the hall cupboard and looked at it.

The bag was not just blue; it was a vivid, clear, electric blue, like a flash of lightning. The regulation colour for schoolbags at his school was a khaki-olive-brown, inside and out, which didn't show stains from when your can of Coke leaked, or when you left your salami sandwiches uneaten and forgot about them for a month.

'I can't take this bag to school,' said Danny. 'Not one this colour. Can't I take my books and stuff in one of those green plastic garbage bags?'

'Certainly not!' said Mrs Hillerey.

On Monday at the bus stop, the kids all stared at the blue bag.

'Hey,' said Jim, who was supposed to be his mate. 'That looks like one of those bags girls take to ballet classes.'

'Hey, Danny, you got one of those frilly dresses in there?' asked Spike.

'Aw, belt up, can't you?' said Danny miserably. On the bus the stirring increased as more and more kids got on. It was a very long trip for Danny. It actually took only twenty minutes – when you had an ordinary brown schoolbag and not a great hunk of sky to carry round with you.

Every time anyone spoke to him they called him 'Little Boy Blue'.

'It matches his lovely blue eyes,' said one kid.

'Maybe he's got a little blue trike with training wheels too,' said another kid.

'Hey, Danny, why didn't you wear some nice blue ribbons in your hair?'

When Danny got off the bus he made a dash for his classroom and shoved the bag under his desk. First period they had Miss Reynolds, and when she was marking the roll she looked along the aisle and saw Danny's bag and said, 'That's a very elegant bag you have there, Danny.'

Everyone else looked around and saw the blue bag and began carrying on. Danny kept a dignified silence, and after five minutes Miss Reynolds made them stop singing *A Life on the Ocean Waves*. But all through Maths and English, heads kept turning round to grin at Danny and his radiantly blue bag.

At morning recess he sneaked into the art room and mixed poster paints into a shade of khaki-olive-brown which he rubbed over his bag with his hankie. When the bell rang he had a grey handkerchief, but the bag was still a clear and innocent blue. 'Darn thing,' Danny muttered in disgust. 'Must be made of some kind of special waterproof atomic material. Nothing sticks to it.'

'What are you doing in the art room, Daniel?' asked Miss Reynolds. 'And what is that terrible painty mess?'

'I was just painting a Zodiac sign on my bag,' said Danny.

'I wish you boys wouldn't write things all over your good schoolbags. Clean up that mess, Danny, and go to your next class.'

But Danny said he was feeling sick and could he please lie down in the sick bay for a while. He sneaked his blue bag in with him, and found the key to the first-aid box and looked inside for something that would turn bright blue bags brown. There was a little bottle of brown lotion, so Danny tipped the whole lot on to cotton wool and scrubbed it into the surface of the bag. But the lotion just ran off the bag and went all over his hands and the bench top in the sick bay.

'Danny Hillerey!' said the school secretary. 'You know very well that no student is allowed to unlock the first-aid box. What on earth are you doing?'

'Sorry,' said Danny. 'Just looking for fruit salts.'

'I think you'd better sit quietly out in the

fresh air if you feel sick,' Mrs Adams said sus-piciously. 'And who owns that peculiar-looking blue bag?'

'It belongs in the sport equipment shed,' said Danny. 'It's got measuring tapes and stuff in it. Blue's our house colour.'

He went and sat outside with the bag shoved under the seat and looked at it and despaired. Kids from his class started going down to the oval for sport, and someone called out 'It's a beautiful blue, but it hasn't a hood.'

Danny glared and said 'Get lost' and 'Drop dead'. Then Miss Reynolds came along and made him go down to the oval with the others.

On the way there Danny sloshed the blue bag in a puddle of mud – but nothing hap-pened, the blue became shinier if anything. He also tried grass stains under the sprinkler, which had the same effect. Amongst the line-up of khaki-olive-brown bags, his blue one was as conspicuous as a Clydesdale horse in a herd of small ponies.

'Hey, Danny, what time's your tap dancing lesson?' said the kids.

'Hey, Danny, where did you get that knitting bag? I want to buy one for my aunty.'

'Hey, Danny, when did you join the Bluebell marching girls' squad?'

Finally Danny had had enough.

'This bag's very valuable if you want to
know,' he said.

'Garn,' everyone scoffed. 'It's just an ordinary old vinyl bag.'

'I had to beg my mum to let me bring that bag to school,' said Danny. 'It took some doing, I can tell you. Usually she won't let it out of the house.'

'Why?' demanded everyone. 'What's so special about it?'

Danny grabbed back his bag and wiped off the traces of mud and poster paint and ulcer lotion and grass stains. The bag was stained inside where all that had seeped in through the seams and the zipper, and it would take some explaining when his mother noticed it. (Which she would, next time she went to spend the weekend at Grandma's.) There was her name inside, E. Hillerey, in big neat letters. E for Enid.

'Well,' said Danny, 'that bag belonged to . . . Well, if you really want to know, it went along on that expedition up Mount Everest.'

Everyone jeered.

'It did so,' said Danny. 'Look, Sir Edm Hillary, there's his name printed right inside. And there's a reason it's thi colour. So it wouldn't get lost in It was the bag Sir Edmund Hillar flag in they stuck up on top of Mount Everest. But I'm not going to bring it to shool any more if all you can do is poke fun at the colour.'

Everyone went all quiet and respectful.

'Gee,' said Jeff in an awed voice, and he touched the letters that Danny's mother had written with a laundry marking pencil.

'Gosh,' said Mark. 'We never knew you were related to that Sir Edmund Hillary.'

Danny looked modest. 'We're only distantly related,' he admitted. 'He's my dad's second cousin.'

'Hey, Danny, can I hold it on the bus? I'll be real careful with it.'

'Hey, Danny, can I have a turn when you bring it to school tomorrow?'

'I'll charge you ten cents a go,' said Danny. 'That's fair, for a bag that went up to the top of Mount Everest.'

'Ten cents a kid,' he calculated. 'One hundred kids at ten cents a turn, ten dollars. A new brown schoolbag. And with a bit of luck, I'll earn all that before someone checks up in the library and finds out Sir Edmund Hillary's name's spelled differently!'

This story is by Robin Klein.

William and the School Report

It was the last day of term. The school had broken up, and William was making his slow and thoughtful way homeward. A casual observer would have thought that William alone among the leaping, hurrying crowd was a true student, that William alone regretted the four weeks of enforced idleness that lay before him. He walked draggingly and as if reluctantly, his brow heavily furrowed, his eyes fixed on the ground. But it was not the thought of the four weeks of holiday that was worrying William. It was a suspicion, amounting almost to a certainty, that he wasn't going to have the four weeks of holiday.

The whole trouble had begun with William's headmaster – a man who was in William's eyes a blend of Nero and Judge Jeffreys and the

Spanish Inquisitioners, but who was in reality a harmless inoffensive man, anxious to do
his duty to the youth entrusted to his care.
William's father had happened to meet him in
the train going up to town, and had asked how
William was getting on. The headmaster had
replied truthfully and sadly that William didn't
seem to be getting on at all. He hadn't, he said,
the true scholar's zest for knowledge, his writing was atrocious and he didn't seem able to
spell the simplest word or do the simplest sum.
Then, brightening, he suggested that William
should have coaching during the holidays. Mr
Parkinson, one of the Junior form masters who
lived near the school, would be at home for the
four weeks, and had offered to coach backward
boys. An hour a day. It would do William, said
the headmaster enthusiastically, all the good in
the world. Give him, as it were, an entirely new
start. Nothing like individual coaching. Nothing at all. William's father was impressed. He
saw four peaceful weeks during which William,
daily occupied with his hour of coaching and
its complement of homework, would lack both
time and spirit to spread around him that
devastation that usually marked the weeks
of the holiday. He thanked the headmaster

190

profusely, and said that he would let him know definitely later on.

William, on being confronted with the suggestion, was at first speechless with horror. When he found speech it was in the nature of a passionate appeal to all the powers of justice and fair dealing.

'In the *holidays*,' he exclaimed wildly. 'There's *lors* against it. I'm sure there's *lors* against it. I've never heard of *anyone* having lessons in the holidays. Not *anyone*! I bet even *slaves* didn't have lessons in the holidays. I bet if they knew about it in Parliament, there'd be an inquest about it. Besides I shall only get ill with overworkin' an' get brain fever same as they do in books, an' then you'll have to pay doctors' bills an' p'raps,' darkly, 'you'll have to pay for my funeral too. I don't see how *anyone* could go on workin' like that for months an' *months* without ever stoppin' once an' not get brain fever and die of it. Anyone'd think you *wanted* me to die. An' if I did die I shun't be surprised if the judge did something to you about it.'

His father, unmoved by this dark hint, replied, coolly, 'I'm quite willing to risk it.'

'An' I don't like Mr Parkinson,' went on William gloomily, 'he's always cross.'

'Perhaps I can arrange it with one of the others,' said Mr Brown.

'I don't like any of them,' said William, still more gloomily, 'they're all always cross.'

He contemplated his wrongs in silence for a few minutes, then burst out again passionately;

''T'isn't as if you weren't makin' me pay for that window. It's not fair payin' for it *an'* havin' lessons in the holidays.'

'It's nothing to do with the window,' explained Mr Brown wearily.

'I bet it is,' said William darkly. 'What else is it if it's not for the window? I've not done anythin' else lately.'

'It's because your work at school fails to reach a high scholastic standard,' said Mr Brown in a tone of ironical politeness.

'How d'you know?' said William after a moment's thought. 'How d'you know it does? You've not seen my report. We don't get 'em till the last day.'

'Your headmaster told me so.'

'Ole Markie?' said William. 'Well,' indignantly, 'I like that. I *like* that. He doesn't teach me at all. He doesn't teach me anythin' at all. I bet he was jus' makin' it up for somethin' to say to you. He'd got to say somethin' an' he couldn't think of anythin' else to say. I bet he tells everyone he meets that their son isn't doing well at school jus' for somethin' to say. I bet he's got a sort of habit of saying it to everyone he meets an' does it without thinkin'.'

'All right,' said William's father firmly. 'I'll

make no arrangements till I've seen your report. If it's a better one than it usually is, of course, you needn't have coaching.'

William felt relieved. There were four weeks before the end of the term. Anything might happen. His father might forget about it altogether. Mr Parkinson might develop some infectious disease. It was even possible, though William did not contemplate the possibility with any confidence, that his report might be better. He carefully avoided any reference to the holidays in his father's hearing. He watched Mr Parkinson narrowly for any signs of incipient illness, rejoicing hilariously one morning when Mr Parkinson appeared with what seemed at first to be a rash but turned out on closer inspection to be shaving cuts. He even made spasmodic effort to display intelligence and interest in class, but his motive in asking questions was misunderstood, and taken to be his usual one of entertaining his friends or holding up the course of the lesson, and he relapsed into his usual state of boredom, lightened by surreptitious games with Ginger. And now the last day of the term had come, and the prospect of holiday coaching loomed ominously ahead. His father had not forgotten. Only last night he had reminded William that it depended on his report whether or not he was to have lessons in the holidays. Mr Parkinson looked almost revoltingly healthy, and in his pocket William carried the worst report he had ever had. Disregarding (in common with the whole school) the headmaster's injunction to give the report to his parents without looking at it first, he had read it apprehensively in the cloakroom and it had justified his blackest fears. He had had wild notions of altering it. The word 'poor' could, he thought, easily be changed to 'good', but few of the remarks stopped at 'poor', and such additions as 'Seems to take no interest at all in this subject' and 'Work consistently ill prepared' would read rather oddly after the comment 'good.'

William walked slowly and draggingly. His father would demand the report, and at once make arrangements for the holiday coaching. The four weeks of the holidays stretched – an arid desert – before him.

'But one hour a day can't spoil the whole holidays, William,' his mother had said, 'you can surely spare one hour out of twelve to improving your mind.'

William had retorted that for one thing his

mind didn't need improving, and anyway it was *his* mind and he was quite content with it as it was, and for another, one hour a day *could* spoil the whole holidays.

'It can spoil it *absolutely*,' he had protested. 'It'll just make every single day of it taste of school. I shan't be able to enjoy myself any of the rest of the day after an hour of ole Parkie an' sums an' things. It'll spoil every *minute* of it.'

'Well, dear,' Mrs Brown had said with a sigh, 'I'm sorry, but your father's made up his mind.'

William's thoughts turned morosely to that conversation as he fingered the long envelope in his pocket. There didn't seem to be any escape. If he destroyed the report and pretended that he had lost it, his father would only write to the school for another, and they'd probably make the next one even more damning to pay him out for giving them extra trouble. The only possibility of escape was for him to have some serious illness, and that, William realized gloomily, would be as bad as the coaching.

To make things worse an aunt of his father's (whom William had not seen for several years) was coming over for the day, and William considered that his family was always more difficult to deal with when there were visitors. Having reached the road in which his home was, he halted irresolute. His father was probably coming home for lunch because of the aunt. He might be at home now. The moment when the report should be demanded was, in William's opinion, a moment to be postponed as far as possible. He needn't go home just yet. He turned aside into a wood, and wandered on aimlessly, still sunk in gloomy meditation, dragging his toes in the leaves.

'If ever I get into Parliament,' he muttered fiercely, 'I'll pass a *lor* against reports.'

He turned a bend in the path and came face to face with an old lady. William felt outraged by the sight of her – old ladies had no right to be in woods – and was about to pass her hurriedly when she accosted him.

'I'm afraid I've lost my way, little boy,' she said breathlessly. 'I was directed to take a short cut from the station to the village through the wood, and I think I must have made a mistake.'

William looked at her in disgust. She was nearly half a mile from the path that was a short cut from the station to the village.

'What part of the village d'you want to

197

get to?' he said curtly.

'Mr Brown's house,' said the old lady, 'I'm expected there for lunch.'

The horrible truth struck William. This was his father's aunt, who was coming over for the day. He was about to give her hasty directions, and turn to flee from her, when he saw that she was peering at him with an expression of delighted recognition.

'But it's William,' she said. 'I remember you quite well. I'm your Aunt Augusta. What a good thing I happened to meet you, dear! You can take me home with you.'

William was disconcerted for a moment. They were in reality only a very short distance from his home. A path led from the part of the wood where they were across a field to the road where the Browns' house stood. But it was no part of William's plan to return home at once. He'd decided to put off his return as far as possible, and he wasn't going to upset his arrangements for the sake of anyone's aunt, much less his father's.

He considered the matter in frowning silence for a minute, then said:

'All right. You c'n come along with me.'

'Thank you, my dear boy,' said the old

lady brightening. 'Thank you. That will be *very* nice. I shall quite enjoy having a little talk with you. It's several years since I met you, but, of course, I recognized you at once.'

William shot a suspicious glance at her, but it was evident that she intended no personal insult. She was smiling at him benignly.

She discoursed brightly as William led her further and further into the heart of the wood and away from his home. She told him stories of her far off childhood, describing in great detail her industry and obedience and perseverance and love of study. She had evidently been a shining example to all her contemporaries.

'There's no joy like the joy of duty done, dear boy,' she said. 'I'm sure that *you* know that.'

'Uh-huh,' said William shortly.

As they proceeded on into the wood, however, she grew silent and rather breathless.

'Are we – nearly there, dear boy?' she said.

They had almost reached the end of the wood, and another few minutes would have brought them out into the main road, where a bus would take them to within a few yards of William's home. William still had no intention of going home, and he felt a fierce resentment against his companion. Her chatter had prevented his giving his whole mind to the problem that confronted him. He felt sure that there was a solution if only he could think of it.

He sat down abruptly on a fallen tree and said casually:

'I'm afraid we're lost. We must've took the wrong turning. This wood goes on for miles an' miles. People've sometimes been lost for days.'

'With – with no food?' said Aunt Augusta faintly.

'Yes, with no food.'

'B–but, they must have died surely?'

'Yes,' said William, 'quite a lot of 'em were dead when they found 'em.'

Aunt Augusta gave a little gasp of terror.

William's heart was less stony than he liked to think. Her terror touched him and he relented.

'Look here,' he said, 'I think p'raps that path'll get us out. Let's try that path.'

'No,' she panted. 'I'm simply exhausted. I can't walk another step just now. Besides it might only take us further into the heart of the wood.'

'Well, I'll go,' said William. 'I'll go an' see if it leads to the road.'

'No, you *certainly* mustn't,' said Aunt
Augusta sharply, 'we must at all costs keep
together. You'll miss your way and we shall
both be lost separately. I've read of that happening in books. People lost in forests and one
going on to find the way and losing the others.
No I'm certainly not going to risk that. I *forbid*
you going a yard without me, William, and I'm
too much exhausted to walk any more just at
present.'

William, who had by now tired of the
adventure and was anxious to draw it to an
end as soon as possible, hesitated, then said
vaguely:

'Well . . . s'pose I leave some sort of trail
same as they do in books.'

'But what can you leave a trail of?' said
Aunt Augusta.

Suddenly William's face shone as if illumi-
nated by a light within. He only just prevented
himself from turning a somersault into the middle of a blackberry bush.

'I've got an envelope in my pocket,' he
said. 'I'll tear that up. I mean—' he added
cryptically, 'it's a case of life and death, isn't
it?'

'Do be careful then, dear boy,' said Aunt

Augusta anxiously. 'Drop it every *inch* of the way. I hope it's something you can spare, by the way?'

'Oh yes,' William assured her, 'it's something I can spare all right.'

He took the report out of his pocket, and began to tear it into tiny fragments. He walked slowly down the path, dropping the pieces, and taking the precaution of tearing each piece into further fragments as he dropped it. There must be no possibility of its being rescued and put together again. Certain sentences, for instance the one that said, 'uniformly bad. Has made no progress at all,' he tore up till the paper on which they were written was almost reduced to its component elements.

The path led, as William had known it would, round a corner and immediately into the main road. He returned a few minutes later, having assumed an expression of intense surprise and delight.

'S'all right,' he announced, 'the road's jus' round there.'

Aunt Augusta took out a handkerchief and mopped her brow.

'I'm so glad, dear boy,' she said. 'So very glad. What a relief! I was just wondering how one told edible from inedible berries. We might, as you said, have been here for days . . . Now let's just sit here and rest a few minutes before we go home. Is it far by the road?'

'No,' said William. 'There's a bus that goes all the way.'

He took his seat by her on the log, trying to restrain the exuberant expansiveness of his grin. His fingers danced a dance of triumph in his empty pockets.

'I was so much relieved, dear boy,' went on Aunt Augusta, 'to see you coming back again. It would have been so terrible if we'd lost each other. By the way, what was the paper that you tore up, dear? Nothing important, I hope?'

William had his face well under control by now.

'It was my school report,' he said, 'I was jus' takin' it home when I met you.'

He spoke sorrowfully as one who has lost his dearest treasure.

Aunt Augusta's face registered blank horror.

'You – you tore up your school report?' she said faintly.

'I had to,' said William, 'I'd rather,' he went on, assuming an expression of noble self-sacrifice, 'I'd rather, lose my school report than have you starve to death.'

It was clear that, though Aunt Augusta was deeply touched by this, her horror still remained.

'But – your school report, dear boy,' she said. 'It's dreadful to think of your sacrificing that for me. I remember so well the joy and pride of the moment when I handed my school report to my parents. I'm sure you know that moment well.'

William, not knowing what else to do, heaved a deep sigh.

'Was it,' said Aunt Augusta, still in a tone of deep concern and sympathy, 'was it a *specially* good one?'

'We aren't allowed to look at them,' said William unctuously; 'they always tell us to take them straight home to our parents without looking at them.'

'Of course. Of course,' said Aunt Augusta. 'Quite right, of course, but – oh, how disappointing for you, dear boy. You have some idea no doubt what sort of a report it was?'

'Oh yes,' said William, 'I've got some sort of an idea all right.'

'And I'm sure, dear,' said Aunt Augusta, 'that it was a very, very good one.'

William's expression of complacent modesty was rather convincing.

'Well . . . I – I dunno,' he said self-consciously.

'I'm sure it was,' said Aunt Augusta. 'I know it was. And *you* know it was really. I can tell that, dear boy, from the way you speak of it.'

'Oh . . . I dunno,' said William, intensifying the expression of complacent modesty that was being so successful. 'I dunno . . . '

'And that tells me that it was,' said Aunt
Augusta triumphantly, 'far more plainly than
if you said it was. I like a boy to be modest
about his attainments. I don't like a boy to go
about boasting of his successes in school. I'm
sure you never do that, do you, dear boy?'

'Oh no,' said William with perfect truth.
'No, I never do that.'

'But I'm so worried about the loss of your
report. How quietly and calmly you sacrificed
it.' It was clear that her appreciation of William's
nobility was growing each minute. 'Couldn't
we try to pick up the bits on our way to the road
and piece them together for your dear father to
see?'

'Yes,' said William. 'Yes, we could try'n
do that.'

He spoke brightly, happy in the conscious-
ness that he had torn up the paper into such
small pieces that it couldn't possibly be put
together.

'Let's start now, dear, shall we?' said Aunt
Augusta; 'I'm quite rested.'

They went slowly along the little path that
led to the road.

Aunt Augusta picked up the 'oo' of 'poor' and

said, 'This must be a "good" of course,' and she
picked up the 'ex' of 'extremely lazy and inat-
tentive' and said. 'This must be an "excellent"
of course,' but even Aunt Augusta realized that
it would be impossible to put together all the
pieces.

I'm afraid it can't be done, dear,' she said
sadly. 'How *disappointing* for you. I feel so
sorry that I mentioned it at all. It must have
raised your hopes.'

'No, it's quite all right,' said William, 'it's
quite all right. I'm not disappointed. Really I'm
not.'

'I *know* what you're feeling, dear boy,'
said Aunt Augusta. 'I know what I should feel
myself in your place. And I hope – I *hope* that
I'd have been as brave about it as you are.'

William, not knowing what to say, sighed
again. He was beginning to find his sigh rather
useful. They had reached the road now. A bus
was already in sight. Aunt Augusta hailed it,
and they boarded it together. They completed
the journey to William's house in silence. Once
Aunt Augusta gave William's hand a quick surreptitious pressure of sympathy and whispered:

'I know *just* what you are feeling, dear boy.'

William, hoping that she didn't, hastily

composed his features to their expression of complacent modesty, tinged with deep disappointment – the expression of a boy who has had the misfortune to lose a magnificent school report.

His father was at home, and came to the front door to greet Aunt Augusta.

'Hello!' he said. 'Picked up William on the way?'

He spoke without enthusiasm. He wasn't a mercenary man, but this was his only rich unmarried aunt, and he'd hoped that she wouldn't see too much of William on her visit.

Aunt Augusta at once began to pour out a long and confused account of her adventure.

'And we were *completely* lost . . . right in the heart of the wood. I was too much exhausted to go a step farther, but this dear boy went on to explore and, solely on my account because I was nervous of our being separated, he tore up his school report to mark the trail. It was, of course, a great sacrifice for the dear boy, because he was looking forward with such pride and pleasure to watching you read it.'

William gazed into the distance as if he saw neither his father nor Aunt Augusta. Only so

could he retain his expression
of patient suffering.

'Oh, he was, was he?'
said Mr Brown sardonically,
but in the presence of his aunt
forebore to say more.

During lunch, Aunt Augusta,
who had completely forgotten her
exhaustion and was beginning to
enjoy the sensation of having been
lost in a wood, enlarged upon the
subject of William and the lost
report.

'Without a word and solely in
order to allay my anxiety, he gave
up what I know to be one of the
proudest moments one's schooldays
have to offer. I'm not one of those
people who forget what it is to be
a child. I can see myself now handing
my report to my mother and father
and watching their faces radiant with
pride and pleasure as they read it. I'm
sure that is a sight that you have often
seen, dear boy?'

William, who was finding his
expression of virtue hard to

sustain under his father's gaze, took refuge in a prolonged fit of coughing which concentrated Aunt Augusta's attention upon him all the more.

'I *do* hope he hasn't caught a cold in that nasty damp wood,' she said anxiously. 'He took *such* care of me and I shall never forget the sacrifice he made for me.'

'*Was* it a good report, William?' said Mrs Brown with tactless incredulity.

William turned to her an expressionless face.

'We aren't allowed to look at 'em,' he said virtuously. 'He tells us to bring 'em home without lookin' at 'em.'

'But I could tell it was a good report,' said Aunt Augusta. 'He wouldn't admit it but I could *tell* that he *knew* it was a good report. He bore it very bravely but I saw what a grief it was to him to have to destroy it—' Suddenly her face beamed. 'I know, I've got an idea! Couldn't you write to the headmaster and ask for a duplicate?'

William's face was a classic mask of horror.

'No, don't do that,' he pleaded, 'don't do that. I-I-I,' with a burst of inspiration, 'I shun't like to give 'em so much trouble in the holidays.'

Aunt Augusta put her hand caressingly on his stubbly head. '*Dear* boy,' she said.

William escaped after lunch, but, before he joined the Outlaws, he went to the wood and ground firmly into the mud with his heel whatever traces of the torn report could be seen.

It was tea-time when he returned. Aunt Augusta had departed. His father was reading a book by the fire. William hovered about uneasily for some minutes.

Then Mr Brown, without raising his eyes from his book, said, 'Funny thing, you getting lost in Croome Wood, William. I should have thought you knew every inch of it. Never been lost in it before, have you?'

'No,' said William, and then after a short silence:

'I say . . . father.'

'Yes,' said Mr Brown.

'Are you – are you really goin' to write for another report?'

'What sort of a report actually *was* the one you lost?' said Mr Brown fixing him with a gimlet eye. 'Was it a very bad one?'

William bore the gimlet eye rather well.

'We aren't allowed to look at 'em, you know,' he said again innocently. 'I told you

211

we're told to bring 'em straight home without looking at 'em.'

Mr Brown was silent for a minute. As I said before, he wasn't a mercenary man, but he couldn't help being glad of the miraculously good impression that William had made on his only rich unmarried aunt.

'I don't believe,' he said slowly, 'that there's the slightest atom of doubt, but I'll give you the benefit of it all the same.'

William leapt exultantly down the garden and across the fields to meet the Outlaws.

They heard him singing a quarter of a mile away.

This story is by Richmal Crompton.

Fabric Crafts

Alastair MacIntyre gripped his son Blair by the throat and shook him till his eyes bulged.

'Look here, laddie,' he hissed. 'I'm warning ye. One more time, say that one more time and whatever it is ye think ye're so good at, *whatever*, I'll have ye prove it!'

'You let go of Blair at once,' said Helen MacIntyre. 'His breakfast's getting cold on the table.'

Giving his son one last fierce shake, Alastair MacIntyre let go. Blair staggered backwards and caught his head against the spice shelf. Two or three little jars toppled over and the last of the turmeric puffed off the shelf and settled gently on his dark hair.

Alastair MacIntyre heard the crack of his son's head against the wood and looked up in anguish.

'Did ye hear that? Did ye hear that, Helen?

He banged his head on yon shelf. He couldnae have done that a week back. The laddie's still growing! It'll be new trousers in another month. Och, I cannae bear it, Helen! I cannae bear to watch him sprouting out of a month's wages in clothes before my eyes. I'd raither watch breakfast telly!'

And picking up his plate, he left the room.

Blair fitted his long legs awkwardly under the table and rubbed his head.

'What was all that about?' he asked his mother. 'Why did he go berserk? What happened?'

'You said it again.'

'I didnae!'

'You did.'

'How? When?'

'You came downstairs, walked through the door, came up behind me at the stove, looked over my shoulder at the bacon in the pan, and you said it.'

'I didnae!'

'You did, lamb. You said: "I bet I could fit more slices of bacon into the pan than that." That's what you said. That's when he threw himself across the kitchen to throttle you.'

'I didnae hear myself.'

Helen MacIntyre put her hands on her son's

shoulders and raised herself on
to her tiptoes. She tried to
blow the turmeric off his hair,
but she wasn't tall enough.

'No. You don't hear yourself.
And you don't think before you
speak either. I reckon all your
fine brains are draining away
into your legs.'

'Blair doesnae have any
brains.' Blair's younger sister,
Annie, looked up from her
crunchy granola. 'If he had
any brains, he wouldnae
say the things he does.'

'I dinnae say them,' Blair
argued. 'They just come out.
I dinnae even hear them when
they're said!'

'There you are,' Annie
crowed. 'That's what Mum
said. All legs, no brain.'

She pushed her plate away
across the table and dumped
her schoolbag in its place. 'Tuesday. Have I
got everything I need? Swimsuit, gym–shorts,
metalwork goggles, flute and embroidery.'

215

'Wheesht!' Blair warned. 'Keep your voice down.' But it was too late. The cheery litany had brought Alastair MacIntyre back into the doorway like the dark avenging angel of some ancient, long-forgotten educational system.

'Are ye quite sure ye've no forgotten anything?' he asked his daughter with bitter sarcasm. 'Skis? Sunglasses? Archery set? Saddle and bridle, perhaps?'

'Och, no!' said Annie. 'I won't be needing any of them till it's our class's turn to go to Loch Tay.'

Alastair MacIntyre turned to his son.

'What about you, laddie? Are you all packed and ready for a long day in school? Climbing boots? Bee-keeping gear? Snorkel and oxygen tank?'

'Tuesday,' mused Blair. 'Only Fabric Crafts.'

'Fabric Crafts?'

'You know,' his wife explained to him. 'Sewing. That useful little skill you never learned.'

'Sewing? A laddie of mine sitting at his desk sewing?'

'Och, no, Dad. We dinnae sit at our desks. We have to share the silks and cottons. We sit round in a circle, and chat.'

'Sit in a circle and sew and chat?'

Blair backed away.

'Mam, he's turning rare red. I hope he's no' going to try again to strangle me!'

Alastair MacIntyre put his head in his hands.

'I cannae believe it,' he said in broken tones. 'My ain laddie, the son and grandson of miners, sits in a sewing circle and chats.'

'I dinnae just chat. I'm very good. I've started on embroidery now I've finished hemming my apron!'

Alastair MacIntyre groaned.

'His apron!'

'Dinnae take on so,' Helen MacIntyre comforted her husband. 'Everyone's son does it. The times are changing.'

She tipped a pile of greasy dishes into the sink and added: 'Thank God.'

'Not *my* son!' Alastair MacIntyre cried. 'Not *my* son! Not embroidery! No! I cannae bear it! I'm a reasonable man. I think I move with the times as fast as the next man. I didnae make a fuss when my ain lassie took up the metalwork. I didnae like it, but I bore with it. But there are limits. A man must have his sticking place, and this is mine. I willnae have my one and only son doing embroidery.'

'Why not?' demanded Blair. 'I'm very good at it. I bet I can embroider much, much better than wee Annie here.'

A terrible silence fell. Then Annie said:

'Ye said it again!'

Blair's eyes widened in horror.

'I didnae!'

'You did. We all heard ye. You said: "I bet I can embroider much, much better than wee Annie here!"'

'I didnae!'

'Ye did.'

'Mam?'

Mrs MacIntyre reached up and laid a comforting hand on his shoulder.

'Ye did, lamb. I'm sorry. I heard it, too.'

Suddenly Alastair MacIntyre looked as if an unpleasant thought had just struck him. He quickly recovered himself and began to whistle casually. He reached over to the draining board and picked up his lunch box. He slid his jacket off the peg behind the door, gave his wife a surreptitious little kiss on the cheek and started sliding towards the back door.

'Dad!'

Alastair MacIntyre pretended not to have heard.

'Hey, *Dad*!'

Even a deaf man would have felt the rever-
berations. Alastair MacIntyre admitted defeat.
He turned back to his daughter.

'Yes, hen?'

'What about what you told him?'

'Who?'

'Blair.'

'What about, hen?'

'About what would happen if he said it again.'

Alastair MacIntyre looked like a hunted animal. He loosened his tie and cleared his throat, and still his voice came out all ragged.

'What did I say?'

'You said: "Say that one more time and whatever it is you think you're so good at, *whatever*, I'll have ye prove it." That's what you said.'

'Och, weel. This doesnae count. The laddie cannae prove he sews better than you.'

'Why not?'

'He just cannae.'

'He can, too. I'm entering my embroidery for the End-of-Term Competition. He can enter his.'

'Och, no, lassie!'

'Yes, Dad. You said so.'

'I was only joking.'

'Och, Dad! You were not!'

Alastair MacIntyre ran his finger around his collar to loosen it, and looked towards his wife for rescue.

'Helen?'

Annie folded her arms over her school bag and looked towards her mother for justice.

'Mam?'

Mrs MacIntyre turned away and slid her arms, as she'd done every morning for the last nineteen years, into the greasy washing-up water.

'I think,' she said, 'it would be very good for him.'

Alastair MacIntyre stared in sheer disbelief at his wife's back. Then he slammed out. The heavy shudder of the door against the wooden frame dislodged loose plaster from the ceiling. Most of it fell on Blair, mingling quite nicely with the turmeric.

'Good for me, nothing,' said Blair. 'I'd enjoy it.'

'I didnae mean good for you,' admitted Mrs MacIntyre. 'I meant it would be good for your father.'

It was with the heaviest of hearts that Alastair MacIntyre returned from the pit head that evening to find his son perched on the doorstep, a small round embroidery frame in one hand, a needle in the other, mastering stem stitch.

'Have ye no' got anything better to do?' he asked his son irritably.

Blair turned his work over and bit off a

221

loose end with practised ease.

'Och, Dad. Ye know I've only got a week. I'm going to have to work night and day as it is.'

Alastair MacIntyre took refuge in the kitchen. To try to cheer himself, he said to Helen:

'Wait till his friends drap in to find him ta'en up wi' yon rubbish. They'll take a rise out o' the laddie that will bring him back into his senses.'

'Jimmy and Iain were here already. He sent them along to The Work Box on Pitlochrie Street to buy another skein of Flaming Orange so he could finish off his border of french knots.'

The tea mug shook in Alastair MacIntyre's hand.

'Och, no,' he whispered.

Abandoning his tea, he strode back into the hall, only to find his son and his friends blocking the doorway as they held one skein of coloured embroidery floss after another up to the daylight.

'Ye cannae say that doesnae match. That's perfect, that is.'

'Ye maun be half blind! It's got a heap more red in it than the other.'

'It has not. It's as yellowy as the one he's run out of.'

'It is not.'

'What about that green, then? That's perfect, right?'

'Aye, that's unco' guid, that match.'

'Aye.'

Clutching his head, Alastair MacIntyre retreated.

The next day, Saturday, he felt better. Ensconced in his armchair in front of the rugby international on the television, his son at his side, he felt a happy man again – till he looked round.

Blair sat with his head down, stitching away with a rather fetching combination of Nectarine and Baby Blue.

'Will ye no' watch the match?' Alastair MacIntyre snapped at his son.

'I am watching,' said Blair. 'You should try watching telly and doing satin stitch. It's no' the easiest thing.'

Alastair MacIntyre tried to put it all out of his mind. France v. Scotland was not a match to spoil with parental disquiet. And when, in the last few moments, the beefy full

back from Dunfermline converted the try that
saved Scotland's bacon, he bounced in triumph
on the springs of his chair and shouted in his
joy:

'Och, did ye see that? Did ye see that!'

'Sorry,' said Blair. 'This coral stitch is the
very de'il. Ye cannae simply stop and look up
half-way through.'

All through the night, Alastair MacIntyre
brooded. He brooded through his Sunday
breakfast and brooded through his Sunday
lunch. He brooded all through an afternoon's
gardening and through most of supper. Then,
over a second helping of prunes, he finally
hatched out a plan.

The next evening, when he drove home
from the pit head, instead of putting the car
away in the garage he parked it in front of
the house – a K-registration Temptress – and
went in search of his wayward son. He found
him on the upstairs landing, fretting to Annie
about whether his cross stitches were correctly
aligned.

'Lay off that, laddie,' Alastair MacIntyre
wheedled. 'Come out and help me tune up
the car engine.'

Blair appeared not to have heard. He held

his work up for his father's inspection.

'What do you reckon?' he said. 'Be honest. Dinnae spare my feelings. Do ye think those stitches in the China Blue are entirely regular? Now look very closely. I want ye to be picky.'

Alastair MacIntyre shuddered. Was this his son? He felt as if an incubus had taken hold of his first born.

'Blair,' he pleaded. 'Come out to the car. I need your help.'

'Take wee Annie,' Blair told him. 'She'll help ye. She got top marks in the car maintenance module. I cannae come.'

'Please, laddie.'

Alastair MacIntyre was almost in tears.

Blair rose. Extended to his full height, he towered over his father.

'Dad,' he said. 'Take wee Annie. I cannae come. I cannae risk getting oil ingrained in my fingers. It'll ruin my work.'

Barely stifling his sob of humiliation and outrage, Alastair MacIntyre took the stairs three at a time on his way down and out to the nearest dark pub.

He came home to find wee Annie leaning over his engine, wiping her filthy hands on an oily rag.

'Ye've no' been looking after it at all well,' she scolded him. 'Your sparking plugs were a disgrace. And how long is it since you changed the oil, I'd like to know.'

Mortified, feeling a man among Martians, Alastair MacIntyre slunk through his own front door and up to his bed.

On the morning of the School Prize-Giving, Alastair MacIntyre woke feeling sick. He got no sympathy from his wife, who lay his suit out on the double bed.

Alastair MacIntyre put his head in his hands.

'I cannae bear it!' he said. 'I cannae bear it. My ain son, winning first prize for Fabric Crafts, for his sewing! I tell you, Helen. I cannae bear it!'

He was still muttering 'I cannae bear it' over and over to himself as the assistant head teacher ushered the two of them to their seats in the crowded school hall. The assistant head teacher patted him on the back in an encouraging fashion and told him: 'You maun be a very proud man today, Mr MacIntyre.'

Alastair MacIntyre sank on to his seat, close to tears.

He kept his eyes closed for most of the ceremony, opening them only when Annie was presented with the Junior Metalwork Prize, a new rasp. Here, to prove he was a man of the times as much as the next fellow, he clapped loudly and enthusiastically, then shut his eyes again directly, for fear of seeing his only son presented with a new pack of needles.

When the moment of truth came, he cracked and peeped. Surreptitiously he peered around at the other parents. Nobody was chortling. Nobody was whispering contemptuously to a neighbour. Nobody was so much as snickering quietly up a sleeve. So when everyone else clapped, he clapped too, so as not to seem churlish.

Somebody leaned forward from the row behind and tapped on his shoulder.

'I wadna say but what ye maun be a proud faither today, Alastair MacIntyre.'

And raw as he was, he could discern no trace of sarcasm in the remark.

As they filed out of the hall, Annie and Blair rejoined them. Alastair MacIntyre congratulated his daughter. He tried to follow up this success by congratulating his son, but the words stuck in his throat. He was rescued by the arrival, in shorts and shirts, of most of the school football team.

'Blair! Are ye no' ready yet? We're waitin' on ye!'

The goalie, a huge burly lad whose father worked at the coal face at Alastair MacIntyre's pit, suddenly reached forward and snatched at Blair's embroidery. Blair's father shuddered. But all the goalie did was to fold it up neatly.

'A fair piece o' work, that,' he said. 'I saw it on display in yon hall. I dinnae ken how ye managed all them fiddly bits.'

'Och, it was nothing,' said Blair. 'I bet if you tried, you could do one just as guid.'

Alastair MacIntyre stared at his son, then his wife, then his daughter, then his son again.

'Och, no,' demurred the goalie. 'I couldnae manage that. I've no' got your colour sense.'

He handed the embroidery to Alastair MacIntyre.

'Will ye keep hold o' that for him,' he said. 'He's got to come and play football now. We cannae wait any longer.' He turned to Annie. 'And you'll have to come too, wee Annie, Neil's awa' sick. You'll have to be the referee.'

Before she ran off, Annie dropped her new rasp into one of her father's pockets. Blair dropped a little packet into the other.

Alastair MacIntyre jumped as if scalded.

'What's in there?' he demanded, afraid to reach in and touch it in case it was a darning mushroom, or a new thimble.

'Iron-on letters,' Blair said. 'I asked for them. They're just the job for football shirts. We learned to iron in Home Economics. I'm going to fit up the whole football team.'

'What with?'

'KIRKCALDY KILLERS,' Blair told him proudly. 'In Flaming Orange and Baby Blue.'

This story is by Anne Fine.

A BASKET OF STORIES FOR SEVEN YEAR OLDS

COLLECTED BY PAT THOMSON

ILLUSTRATED BY RACHEL BIRKETT

Climb into this basket of stories and you will find . . . Charlie and his puppy, a wolf that tells riddles, a witch, a smelly giant, and many other strange and exciting people and animals. You won't want to stop reading until you get right to the bottom of the basket!

'Jam-packed with goodies'

The Sunday Telegraph

'Will be enjoyed by children of all ages'
The Times Educational Supplement

'Will stimulate even the most reluctant reader'

Junior Education

Read Alone or Read Aloud

0 552 52729 7

A SACKFUL OF STORIES FOR EIGHT YEAR OLDS

COLLECTED BY PAT THOMSON

ILLUSTRATED BY PADDY MOUNTER

Delve into this sack of stories and you will find . . . a Martian wearing Granny's jumper, that well-known comic fairy-tale pair Handsel and Gristle, a unicorn, a leprechaun, a princess who is a pig, and many other strange and exciting characters. You won't want to stop reading until you get right to the bottom of the sack!

'There are thirteen stories to a sackful and each and every one is a tried-and-tested cracker'

The Sunday Telegraph

'Will be enjoyed by children of all ages'

The Times Educational Supplement

'Will stimulate even the most reluctant reader'

Junior Education

0 552 52730 0